"I don't belong here."

Ashleigh could hear some of the other
to each other as they saddled their hors
she didn't know greeted Mona, who calle
fully. Ashleigh began to feel a little lone
know the people Mona knew from
lessons. She didn't have a special saddle
She didn't have the right clothes, and n
feel very sure of herself. She was out of p

"I can't do this, Mona," she said qu
belong here."

"What?" Mona peeked under Frisk
stared hard at her. "Of course you can
be right beside you. Come and see
jumping."

Collect all the books in the Ashleigh series:

Ashleigh #1: *Lightning's Last Hope*
Ashleigh #2: *A Horse for Christmas*
Ashleigh #3: *Waiting for Stardust*
Ashleigh #4: *Good-bye, Midnight Wanderer*
Ashleigh #5: *The Forbidden Stallion*
Ashleigh #6: *A Dangerous Ride*
Ashleigh #7: *Derby Day**

ASHLEIGH'S Thoroughbred Collection

Star of Shadowbrook Farm
The Forgotten Filly
Battlecry Forever!

*Coming soon

THOROUGHBRED
Ashleigh

A DANGEROUS RIDE

CREATED BY

JOANNA CAMPBELL

WRITTEN BY

MARY NEWHALL ANDERSON

HarperEntertainment
A Division of HarperCollinsPublishers

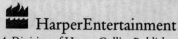

HarperEntertainment

A Division of HarperCollins*Publishers*
10 East 53rd Street, New York, NY 10022-5299

This is a work of fiction. The characters, incidents, and dialogues are products of the author's imagination and are not to be construed as real. Any resemblance to actual events or persons, living or dead, is entirely coincidental.

 Produced by 17th Street Productions, a division of Daniel Weiss Associates, Inc.

ISBN 0-06-106559-5

HarperCollins®, ®, and HarperEntertainment™ are trademarks of HarperCollins Publishers Inc.

Cover art © 1999 by Daniel Weiss Associates, Inc.

First printing: August 1999

Printed in the United States of America

Visit HarperEntertainment on the World Wide Web at
http://www.harpercollins.com

❖ 10 9 8 7 6 5 4 3 2 1

For Joan Diane Kerrigan, and for Blaze and Peco,
who always brought us home safely

1

"Stardust?" ten-year-old Ashleigh Griffen called as she stepped inside the barn, a Ziploc bag of apple pieces in her hand. "Ready to ride?"

Ashleigh's pretty chestnut mare hung her head over her stall door and let out an eager whinny in response. Ashleigh laughed and hurried down the aisle. After being grounded from riding for nearly a month because of a bad math grade, Ashleigh was finally being allowed to get on a horse again. She could hardly wait.

Farther down the barn aisle, she saw her father, Derek Griffen, holding Wanderer, one of the Griffens' prized broodmares. Jonas McIntyre, their stable hand, was crouched down, running his hands over the mare's black legs. Wanderer's new filly, Velvet, stood by the mare's side, watching the humans with deep curiosity, her fuzzy brown ears twitching.

"Is everything okay?" Ashleigh asked. She tucked her long brown hair behind her ears and eyed Wanderer anxiously. Every one of the ten broodmares her parents owned was important to the success of Edgardale, their small breeding farm, but Wanderer was the most valuable. One of Wanderer's colts, nicknamed Slammer, had brought $200,000 at the Keeneland yearling sale last year. But Wanderer had been going through a streak of bad luck: She'd almost died of colic not long ago, and her last colt, Midnight Wanderer, had had to be put down because of a broken leg.

"She's fine," Mr. Griffen said. "We just wanted to check her over."

Mr. Griffen gave Wanderer's shoulder a pat, then nodded to Jonas, who unclipped the mare from the crossties and led her out of the barn.

Ashleigh headed for the storage area, where the wheelbarrow and pitchforks were kept.

"And where do you think you're going?" Mr. Griffen asked, folding his arms across his chest and narrowing his eyes.

Ashleigh's stomach dropped. That morning her parents had told her she wouldn't be grounded anymore. Her father couldn't have forgotten already.

"But I got Bs on my last two math tests, and an A on the last worksheet, remember?" She faltered. "As soon as I get my stalls cleaned I was going to ride."

Her father frowned, and Ashleigh bit her lower lip. He couldn't have changed his mind. She held her breath and waited.

"Cleaning the stalls could be a problem," he finally said.

"Why?" Ashleigh asked.

Her father smiled and winked at her. "Because Jonas and I cleaned them for you."

"You did?" She flung her arms around him. "Thanks, Dad. And I'm not grounded anymore, right? I can ride Stardust?"

"Yes, you can ride," Mr. Griffen said, hugging her back. "Your mother and I are very proud of how hard you've worked on your grades."

"It really helped when Peter Danworth showed me how math can apply to horse things, too," Ashleigh said.

"Then at least one good thing came of your adventure in Florida last month," her father replied.

Ashleigh felt a blush start up her cheeks. She'd been reluctant to leave Stardust and go to Florida to visit thirteen-year-old Peter Danworth and his parents. The Danworths owned Aladdin's Treasure, a beautiful black colt bred at Edgardale. While the Griffens were visiting the Danworths, Ashleigh had sneaked a ride on the racehorse. Even though she had fallen off, it had been a thrilling ride, but it would be a long time before she even thought about disobeying her parents again.

"Aladdin's racing at Keeneland next week, don't forget. We'll get to see for ourselves how fast he's running now," her father said, pulling her thoughts away from her wild ride on the beach.

Keeneland was a racetrack only twenty minutes from Edgardale, and Ashleigh had been to lots of races there. "I can't wait," she said. "I want to go to the track every day to see him."

Ashleigh wanted to be a jockey, and she loved racing more than anything. She watched nearly every race aired on TV, but nothing compared to seeing a race live. A pack of sleek and powerful Thoroughbreds bursting from the gate as the bell sounded, their legs working like pistons as they thundered around the track . . . jockey and horse working in unison to win the race and set a new record . . . the roar of the crowd as one horse found yet another gear, surged ahead, and ran its heart out down to the wire . . . Ashleigh could watch a race every day of her life and never tire of it. And one day she would be racing herself.

"Don't worry," her father said. "We won't miss a minute with Aladdin. Now go and get Stardust. You've been out of the saddle long enough—I bet you can't wait to gallop."

"Thanks, Dad!" Ashleigh said, and hurried down the aisle to Stardust's stall.

Stardust was dozing, her head hanging low in the shaft of spring sunshine streaming through her stall window. When Ashleigh called her name, the chestnut mare's head popped up and she whickered softly. Ashleigh fed her some apple pieces, then slipped her halter on and led the mare out into the aisle.

She put Stardust in crossties and got the bucket of grooming tools from the tack room.

"It won't take long to get you ready to go," she said, picking up a brush. Stardust's copper-colored coat already glistened like a new penny. Even though she hadn't been able to ride, Ashleigh had groomed her mare every day.

Stardust gave her a nudge, and Ashleigh laughed. "You want to get out and go as much as I do, don't you?"

She settled her saddle on Stardust's back and tightened the girth. When she put the bridle on, Stardust took the bit willingly. Ashleigh fastened the throat latch, then slipped her helmet on and buckled it, and led Stardust outside.

She swung into the saddle, taking a moment to relish the wonderful feeling of being back on her horse. Stardust pawed the ground impatiently, and Ashleigh picked up the reins. "Let's go," she said, heading the mare down the drive. The mare seemed as happy as Ashleigh to be riding after so long. She bobbed her head, danced, snorted at nothing, and pulled at the bit, telling Ashleigh she wanted to move out.

"You sure are feeling your oats," Ashleigh said as Stardust fought the bit. Ashleigh pressed her heels down, making sure her seat was steady. She didn't want to come off Stardust her first day back in the saddle. Stardust pranced sideways a few steps, and Ashleigh laughed and patted the mare's neck. "Take it easy, silly. Let's get warmed up before we do any galloping."

They turned at the road and headed toward the Gardeners' farm, next door to Edgardale. Ahead of them Ashleigh noticed a white plastic bag caught in a bush beside the road. She tightened her grip on Stardust's reins and rode toward the bag. The previous winter Stardust had spooked at lots of little things, but with work she had gotten much better. But after a month of not being ridden, Ashleigh didn't know how Stardust would behave around the piece of garbage.

As they neared it, a slight breeze caught the bag, sending it fluttering to the ground. Stardust's ears snapped forward. She whipped her head up and started to wheel around, ready to flee back to Edgardale. Ashleigh caught her breath, gripped with her knees, and brought Stardust's head back around. For a moment Stardust trembled beneath her.

Ashleigh stroked the mare's shoulder. "It's okay, girl," she reassured the nervous horse. "It's just garbage, not a monster. It isn't going to eat you."

As she talked, Stardust started to relax. When she finally dropped her head from its tense, alert position, Ashleigh breathed a sigh of relief. She urged Stardust past the plastic bag. The mare kept a watchful eye on it, but she didn't spook again.

Ashleigh looked for other things that might startle her horse farther along the road, but soon she felt herself relax, too. She couldn't stop the happy smile that stretched across her face. With winter behind them, there would be lots of great riding weather in the weeks to come. And now that spring had finally arrived, summer was not far behind.

Ashleigh loved springtime, when all the new foals were on the ground with their gangly legs, soft coats, and wide eyes. But summer had to be the best, with long days of beautiful weather. She loved to watch the foals, strong and curious, playing in the paddocks and racing around their placid mothers. Best of all, summer meant hours and hours every day just for riding.

She turned Stardust at the Gardeners' driveway and rode past the pasture where Mrs. Gardener's big gray hunter, Orion, stood in the afternoon sun. The horse looked up, whickering softly as they passed, and then went back to grazing.

Before Ashleigh and her best friend, Mona Gardener, had horses, Ashleigh had ridden Moe, her family's little part-Shetland pony, and Mona had ridden her Welsh pony, Silver. But Mona's parents had given her a Thoroughbred mare for Christmas that year, and Mona had leased Silver to a little girl on the other side of town.

Mona stood with Frisky, her gorgeous bay mare with four white stockings, in front of the Gardeners' barn. She waved at Ashleigh and swung onto Frisky's back.

"Come on," she called. "You have to see the great jumps my dad put up."

Ashleigh urged Stardust into a trot. During the winter Mona had started jumping lessons along with Jamie Wilson and Lynne Duran, two of their classmates. Ashleigh would rather race than jump, but if everyone else was jumping, she'd be left out if she didn't try it. And as soon as she had a look at Mona's jumps, they could get out and gallop on the trails.

She followed Mona and Frisky to a paddock near the barn. At one end of the paddock Mrs. Gardener had some jumps set up to use with Orion. Closer to the barn, Mr. Gardener had set up four sets of wooden Xs. He had propped white painted poles in the center of each pair of braces to make a series of jumps that were only about two feet high, much lower than the jumps Mrs. Gardener used.

"What are those for?" Ashleigh pointed at several poles lying on the ground, spaced about five feet apart.

"Cavaletti poles," Mona said. "I trot Frisky over them after I do the warm-up exercises my trainer showed me."

Ashleigh watched Mona ask Frisky to bend her neck to the right several times, then to the left. She started to do the same with Stardust. As soon as she picked up the right rein, Stardust brought her nose around. The mare was almost as flexible to the left. Ashleigh rubbed Stardust's sleek shoulder and had her stretch her neck a few more times.

"Now what?" she asked Mona, leaning forward to hug Stardust. She could hardly wait to get out of the paddock and go for a gallop.

But Mona started circling Frisky around the paddock at a walk. "We need to finish warming up," she said.

Ashleigh and Stardust joined her, and they rode side by side.

"Have you decided on your project for the school science fair yet?" Mona asked.

Ashleigh sighed. "No. I'll never come up with anything as good as Barry Donovan's weather station. He's going to get grand champion for sure."

Mona nodded. "I know," she said. "I only hope my seed-growing project is good enough for a blue ribbon." She pushed Frisky into a trot.

Ashleigh asked Stardust for more speed, and the girls posted in time to the horses' gaits. "Your project is great," Ashleigh reassured Mona. "I wish I'd thought of it."

Mona gave Ashleigh a sideways look. "You needed to start a couple of weeks ago," she said, turning Frisky.

Ashleigh and Stardust stayed even with Mona and Frisky, not missing a step when they changed directions. "I know," Ashleigh said, then grinned. "I probably would have forgotten to water the seedlings, anyway. I'll get a book at the library tomorrow and find something over the weekend."

Mona slowed Frisky to a fast walk. "Have you heard anything from the Danworths about how Aladdin is doing?" she asked.

Ashleigh slowed Stardust to keep pace with Frisky. "He ran really well in his last two races. And he's coming up to Keeneland soon—I can't wait." Aladdin had been running badly when the Griffens went to see him in Florida, but Ashleigh had discovered the trick to making the colt run his best.

"It's so cool that you were the one to figure out what was slowing him down," Mona said. "But I still don't see how that thing on his noseband could have changed everything."

"You mean the shadow roll," Ashleigh said. "It makes him drop his head, so his gait smooths out. Then he can stretch out and run."

"And Aladdin really can move," Mona said, her voice full of admiration.

"So, what do we do next?" Ashleigh asked, gazing toward the field beyond the Gardeners' house. Now that Stardust was well warmed up and listening to her, she wanted to get out of the paddock and *run*.

"Now we go over the cavaletti poles," Mona said, leading the way to the row of poles on the ground.

Ashleigh pulled her attention back to the paddock. She watched as Mona rose in the saddle and slipped her hands up Frisky's neck. Frisky trotted easily over the poles. When they crossed the last one, Mona sat down again.

"That doesn't look so tough," Ashleigh said, heading Stardust for the poles and mimicking Mona's position. Stardust trotted briskly over the cavaletti. Ashleigh sat down when they had cleared the last pole. "So far so good," she said to Mona with a grin. "Now what?"

"Okay, watch this," Mona said, turning Frisky toward the center of the paddock. Ashleigh watched closely as Mona cued her mare into a canter and headed toward one of the jumps. As Ashleigh watched, they popped over the low rail. It didn't look very difficult. She watched Mona and Frisky go over the other rails, looking better with each jump.

Then Mona trotted Frisky to where Ashleigh waited with Stardust. "Your turn," she said, patting Frisky's neck.

"Okay," Ashleigh said. She had jumped Stardust over logs and brush piles higher than these rails. Confident, she headed Stardust toward the first jump. She sat up and kept a firm hold on the reins, prepared in case Stardust refused or tried to run out.

But Stardust seemed comfortable around the white rail jumps. Ashleigh kept her at a trot and moved into what felt like a good jumping position. She felt the mare adjust her stride as they approached the jump. Stardust popped over the pole easily, but she landed with a bounce, sending Ashleigh forward on her neck. Stardust turned and headed for the second jump right away, throwing Ashleigh off balance. Ashleigh gripped with her legs and grabbed the mare's mane to keep from slipping off. She pushed herself upright and gritted her teeth, pulling Stardust in a little before they reached the next jump.

At the second fence their takeoff felt better and they landed neatly. Ashleigh didn't bounce quite as far out of the saddle, and she quickly settled back into place and guided Stardust toward the next jump. By the time they finished the little course and rode back to Mona and Frisky, Ashleigh felt more sure of herself.

"That wasn't so bad," she said, grinning at Mona.

They took turns going over the jumps a few more times. Each time it got easier, and Ashleigh started approaching the jumps at a canter. She quickly figured out how to control Stardust's approach, until she was making the rounds of the four jumps almost as easily as Mona.

"Do you want to ride the course together?" Mona asked.

Ashleigh looked at the horses. Frisky was nuzzling Stardust's shoulder. "I don't think they'd mind," she said. "Let's try it."

They took the mares around at a trot, to give them a chance to get used to jumping together. Ashleigh flashed a quick look at Mona as they cleared the first jump. Mona grinned back, and they headed for the second rail, still in stride. Jumping alone was okay, but riding beside Mona was great. The two mares finished together, and Ashleigh brought Stardust to a stop.

Mona and Frisky stopped beside them. "That was fun!" Mona breathed.

"Let's try it again," Ashleigh said eagerly, turning Stardust toward the jumps once more.

They rode the course again, keeping the horses in stride, side by side. The bay and chestnut mares seemed to understand the girls' commands perfectly, soaring over the jumps in unison each time.

"Ash, we have got to try them in a pairs class. They'd be awesome!" Mona exclaimed when they had finished the course.

"You mean at a show?" Ashleigh said breathlessly. "I don't think so, Mona. I've never been to a horse show in my life."

"Well, you'd be great," Mona said, and added, "I'm going to one this weekend, you know."

"I just don't think I'm up for it, Mona. Sorry," Ashleigh said, smiling. "But let's try the course again—the other way this time."

When they were finished Ashleigh noticed the sun hovering low on the treetops beyond the paddock fence, and realized it was getting late. "I have to get home," she said, disappointed. "We don't have time for a trail ride now."

"Sorry," Mona said. "I guess we got carried away. We'll go for a trail ride tomorrow," she promised.

"Okay. I'll see you at school," Ashleigh called, and headed Stardust for the gate. She rode home slowly, relishing the feel of being on Stardust's back once more as they moved through the fields of lush Kentucky bluegrass.

Back at Edgardale, Ashleigh untacked Stardust and put her away, giving the mare a flake of hay and a can of grain before hurrying up to the house.

When she sat down at the dinner table, she was still thinking about her afternoon. *Jumping is fun, but it isn't the same as racing,* she mused. Jumping was so controlled—nothing could beat a good gallop.

Her thirteen-year-old sister, Caroline, tapped her on the shoulder. "Ash, wake up. I said, 'Pass the mashed potatoes, please,'" she said, tossing her blond hair.

Ashleigh jumped slightly. "Sorry," she said, pausing to scoop a spoonful onto her own plate before passing them on to her sister. She only half listened when five-year-old Rory began to chatter about his day at kindergarten.

"Will you take me and Moe for a ride tomorrow, Ashleigh?" Rory asked while he made a deep depression in his mashed potatoes. "And will you pour some gravy inside my potato volcano?

"Sure," she said, tipping the pitcher of gravy over his plate. Rory watched carefully, his big blue eyes wide. Rory and Caroline shared their mother's blond hair and fair complexion. Ashleigh took after her father's darker coloring.

"Mr. Danworth called this afternoon," her father said.

Ashleigh's head shot up. "What did he say?" she demanded. "Is Aladdin okay?"

"You remember Mike Smith, their trainer, don't you?"

"Of course I do," Ashleigh exclaimed. Mike had been very nice to her during their stay at the Danworths' Florida farm.

"Mike is bringing Aladdin up to Keeneland on Saturday to get him ready for next week's race," Mr. Griffen said. "The Danworths will be coming up later on to watch him race."

"Is Peter coming up, too?" Ashleigh asked excitedly. Although they hadn't started out on very good terms, she and Peter had ended up friends.

Caroline looked up, too. Even though she didn't share Peter's and Ashleigh's love of horses, Caroline and Peter had hit it off from the start. Ashleigh hoped they didn't end up leaving her out of everything they did while the Danworths were in Kentucky.

"He should be," her father said with a nod. "I thought we'd go to the track Saturday," he added, setting a piece of meatloaf on Ashleigh's plate. "I want to see how Aladdin looks."

"Can I go?" Ashleigh asked, spearing a bite of meatloaf with her fork.

"Are you sure you want to go to the track?" Mrs. Griffen asked in a teasing voice.

Mr. Griffen handed a bowl of cooked carrots to Caroline. "Of course you can come, Ashleigh."

Caroline groaned. "Can I stay home? Please? Don't make me hang around the track all day." Although Caroline looked exactly like a younger version of Mrs. Griffen, she might as well have belonged to another family, given how little interest she showed in horses.

Mrs. Griffen glanced at Caroline. "You can stay home with Rory," she relented.

"But I want to go, too," Rory protested.

"We don't want to overwhelm Mike and Aladdin with visitors, Rory," Mrs. Griffen said gently. "I'm sure Caroline would be happy to watch you ride Moe on Saturday, and we'll all go together next weekend to see Aladdin in his race."

"Fine with me," Caroline said, looking relieved.

"Okay," Rory said agreeably.

Since it was Caroline's turn to do the dishes, Ashleigh slipped upstairs to do her homework. She worked quickly through a page of math problems. The work just made so much more sense after the help Peter had given her. She put the math book away, then opened her science book to see if she could figure out a good project for Monday's science fair.

Her Maine coon kitten, Prince Charming, jumped onto her lap and started purring. Ashleigh stroked his fluffy coat as she flipped through the pages. Her mind wandered to the afternoon, to the feel of Stardust carrying her over the jumps. The most fun had been riding side by side with Mona. *What would it be like to ride in a show?* she wondered.

Ashleigh remembered the feel of Aladdin's powerful muscles when she had galloped him on the beach. She'd never wanted to do anything else but be a jockey, to learn to control that strength and speed. Jumping wasn't going to help her do that, was it? Besides, now that Aladdin was going to be at Keeneland, she wanted to be at the track every chance she got. She wouldn't have time to practice jumping and go to horse shows with Mona.

2

Ashleigh raced to the barn Friday after school, eager to get her chores done so she could go riding. All she wanted to do was jump on Stardust and go for a gallop. She cleaned her assigned stalls quickly before bringing her mare in. She had Stardust in crossties and was getting her saddle out when Rory walked into the barn, his arms folded over his chest.

"You told me we'd ride today," he said, his lower lip sticking out in a pout.

Ashleigh eyed her brother's unhappy face. She'd completely forgotten her promise to take Rory and Moe out. "You're right, I did, Rory. And that's what we're going to do." Her gallop on Stardust would just have to wait.

"I'll help you tack up Moe." She pushed her frustration aside and smiled at her brother. Ashleigh wanted to feel Stardust galloping full out. She yearned to feel the wind in her face and the horse's muscles working beneath her. But she didn't want to disappoint Rory. She'd get a chance to gallop—just not as soon as she wanted.

Rory brought the little brown pony in from the paddock while Ashleigh finished tacking up Stardust. It didn't take long to get Moe ready. She held his bridle while Rory strapped on his helmet and swung onto the pony's saddle. He grinned up at Ashleigh as she settled onto Stardust's back.

"Are we ready?" she asked.

Rory nodded happily, and Ashleigh led the way down the lane between the paddocks.

The rolling pastures swept away from the farm like patchwork squares of vivid green, divided by rows of white fencing. The colorful mix of bay, chestnut, and gray mares grazed placidly while their foals dozed in the afternoon sun. Wanderer, the only black mare at Edgardale, was nuzzling her filly.

Rory sat straight in Moe's saddle, his heels down and his hands over the pommel. He and the molasses-colored pony were a perfect pair. Rory pointed at Go Gen's dark foal. "Shadow looks like Aladdin."

"Let's hope she's as fast as her big brother, too," Ashleigh said. "Do you want to go see Midnight's tree?"

"Okay," he said.

Ashleigh urged Stardust into a trot, heading for the spot where they had buried Wanderer's colt. When they reached the solitary seedling she and Rory had planted in the colt's memory, she halted Stardust. A bubble of sorrow caught in her chest, and she swallowed hard to keep it from rising to her throat.

"Ashleigh, look!" Rory pointed at the little tree. "There's a red bird sitting on it. There's a little bird watching over Midnight. He isn't alone at all!"

Ashleigh's mother had taught her the names of some of the types of birds they often saw around the farm. This one was a cardinal. The bird cocked its head and eyed them, then warbled a short song. Ashleigh smiled. The singing bird made her feel better about losing Midnight.

"That's a cardinal, Rory. And you're right—I bet when this tree gets big there'll be lots of nests in it and Midnight will have even more friends. He'd like that."

"I'm glad we planted it for him," Rory said. "Take care of Midnight, Mr. Cardinal."

"Ready to trot home?" Ashleigh asked her little brother.

"Let's go!" Rory cried, and nudged Moe gently with his heels.

Moe's fuzzy ears were pricked as Rory posted to his bouncy short strides. Ashleigh let the pair get ahead before asking Stardust to trot. Soon she had caught up to Moe, and they trotted into the stable yard side by side.

"Don't worry, Ash," Rory said breathlessly as he swung from Moe's saddle. "I can put him away myself." Ashleigh smiled, but nevertheless she stayed around to supervise until Moe was safely back in his stall.

By the time she got to the Gardeners', Mona and Frisky were already in the paddock, hard at work. Ashleigh sat on Stardust just inside the fence, watching Mona closely while she and Frisky went over the jumps. She wanted to see exactly how Mona positioned herself for the takeoff, where she put her hands, and where her seat was when Frisky landed. Ashleigh thought she had done pretty well the day before, but she still had a lot to learn. If she was going to jump with Mona, she wanted to do it right. She wasn't going to just hang on and let Stardust carry her over the fences.

"I'm going to ask Dad to rearrange the jumps next week," Mona said, stopping Frisky beside Ashleigh and Stardust. "I'm afraid Frisky's going to get bored. Maybe Dad will help me put up some other stuff to jump over, too. At the shows the jumps are decorated."

"With what?" Ashleigh asked. She couldn't imagine asking Stardust to go over one of the huge brick walls or stacks of logs she'd seen in jumping magazines.

The simple rails Mr. Gardener had set up were pretty tame compared to a solid, six-foot wall.

"Sometimes they're just fences or poles painted with red stripes, but they have stone-wall oxers, too, and liverpools."

Ashleigh cocked her head and made a face at her friend. "Oxen? Liver? Gross, Mona."

Mona shook her head, giggling. "Oxers, Ash. They're like two jumps close together, so the horse goes over both at once. Like jumping a box. And a liverpool's supposed to be a water jump, but at lots of the shows they just use a blue tarp. Then they have jumps that look like walls or hedges, or they have planks with bright stripes painted on them."

Ashleigh shook her head. "It's amazing that the horses just go over all of that."

Mona grinned. "It's all part of the challenge. Jumping isn't just going over poles, Ashleigh."

"Well, give me a nice oval racetrack any day," Ashleigh said. "Now show me exactly where my hands should be when we take off. Do you always put them up here on her neck?" Ashleigh stood in her stirrups and tried to imitate the jumping position.

Mona nodded. "Just lean forward and get up off the saddle about an inch. I grab a handful of mane so I won't jerk her mouth by accident if we get the distance wrong."

Ashleigh took Stardust over the course of cross rails, trying to perfect her seat and hand position. Stardust sailed easily over the jumps, and Ashleigh smiled to herself. The feeling of rising into the air when they took off was pretty awesome, as was the weightless sensation when they flew over the obstacles.

"You two look really good, Ash," Mona said after Ashleigh had completed the little course.

"I think she likes it," Ashleigh said, leaning forward to rub the mare's ears. "And it is kind of fun."

The girls rode the course together again, taking the jumps side by side. Stardust and Frisky kept the same pace around the paddock, as if they knew what the girls wanted them to do.

Just as Mona had promised, they only spent a little while in the paddock before heading for the trails. But Ashleigh realized she didn't mind the time they had spent practicing. Learning to jump was a new challenge, and Stardust seemed to be having fun.

"I'm going to that horse show tomorrow," Mona said as they headed toward the hill behind the Gardeners' farm. "Are you sure you don't want to come and watch? I think it would be fun if you started showing, too," Mona went on before Ashleigh could answer. They started up the hill. "I know you could do really well, Ash," she added.

The sun was getting low and the air had a little nip to

it, but Ashleigh felt warm from working in the paddock. "I can't. I'm going to Keeneland to see Aladdin," she told her friend. She leaned forward in a jumping position as they climbed the hill. "Otherwise I'd go with you."

When they reached the top, they stopped the horses for a moment. The land fell away around them, and they looked out across fields of green. In many of the pastures they could see horses grazing, but some of the fields had been plowed recently, leaving neat rectangles of dark earth.

"I love Kentucky," Mona said.

"Me too," Ashleigh replied. She pointed toward Edgardale. "That's where my training oval is going to be. Right there, near my stallion barn. I'm going to raise the greatest racehorses to ever run on the track."

Mona squinted. "I see it, Ash," she replied with a giggle. "With a big sign over it that says Ashleigh's Acres."

"That's a great name," Ashleigh said, laughing. She picked up Stardust's reins. "Come on. Let's go!" she called, squeezing her calves into the horse's sides and pressing Stardust into a canter.

They cantered across the field to the start of one of their favorite trails, where they urged the mares faster, into a gallop. The wind whipped Ashleigh's face and the sound of pounding hooves filled her head. She felt Stardust's muscles work beneath her, and she leaned forward, pressing her fists against Stardust's neck.

Ashleigh could have galloped on forever, but daylight was starting to fade. She and Mona turned the horses and walked them toward home.

"Actually, there's another jumping show Sunday afternoon," Mona said as they neared the Gardeners' barn. "If things go well tomorrow, I want to go to that one, too. Mom and Dad said it would be fine as long as Frisky is okay. Maybe you could come with us then?" she asked.

"Well, I'd go to watch you ride," Ashleigh said. "But I just don't think I'm ready to take Stardust to a show. Not yet."

Mona shrugged. "Give me a call tomorrow," she said.

They parted ways when they reached the barn. Ashleigh waved good-bye and headed down the drive. As she rode she tried to imagine herself riding Stardust over jumps at a horse show. But the image was soon replaced by daydreams of racing Aladdin across the sand. And the very next day she'd get to see the magnificent black stallion once more!

On Saturday morning when Ashleigh woke up, the dark sky was fading to blue and birds were chirping outside her window. She threw back the covers and bounced out of bed.

"Saturday, Saturday, I love Saturday!" she sang as she began to get dressed.

Caroline rolled to face the wall and pulled the blankets over her head. "Be quiet," she grumbled, hunching down under the covers. "I'm trying to sleep."

"This is the best part of the day," Ashleigh said, shaking her head in disgust. She dressed quickly and hurried down to the barn. Her father and Jonas were letting the mares and foals out for the day.

Ashleigh stopped at Stardust's stall. The mare hung her head over the door, and Ashleigh ran her hand along the white stripe down Stardust's face. "Hey, girl, do you want to run this afternoon," she asked, "or do you want to jump?" Stardust flipped her nose up and down, making Ashleigh laugh. "You want to do both?" She slipped on Stardust's halter and turned the mare out in the paddock with Moe. Then she headed back to the barn to help her father and Jonas.

"You can bring Marvy Mary out, Ashleigh," Mr. Griffen said as he led Althea down the aisle. Althea's foal, a chestnut like her dam, pranced alongside. Although she wore a tiny halter, Mr. Griffen didn't have a lead line on her. The filly wasn't about to leave her mother's side.

Ashleigh clipped a lead to Marvy Mary's halter and

led the shiny bay mare from her stall. As they walked from the barn, Marvy's colt stuck to his dam's side like a magnet on metal.

Finally the mares and foals were in their paddocks. Ashleigh cleaned her assigned stalls one by one and hurried back to the house for breakfast.

Caroline was buttering toast when Ashleigh came inside. Her blond hair hung over her eyes and her bathrobe hung loose, the belt dragging on the floor. "I don't suppose you went ahead and cleaned all my stalls while you were at it, did you?" Caroline asked. She swept her hair away with the back of her hand and gave Ashleigh a hopeful look.

"Oh, no," Ashleigh said, peeling a banana. "There's plenty left for you and Rory to do."

Caroline wrinkled her nose. "Thanks, Ash."

Ashleigh washed the breakfast dishes and ran upstairs to change her clothes. When she was ready she raced back downstairs. She could hardly stand to wait, knowing Aladdin was already at Keeneland, but her parents seemed to take forever to get ready to leave for the track. When they finally walked out of the house, Ashleigh hurried ahead of them and climbed into the car.

"If you need anything, Jonas is at the barn," Mrs. Griffen told Caroline as she opened the car door. "And don't forget you told Rory you'd help him ride."

"We'll be fine," Caroline assured their mother. She and Rory waved good-bye from the porch.

Before long they were passing the Bluegrass Airport, just down the road from the Keeneland track. Ashleigh gazed out the window as her father turned onto the racetrack grounds and headed for the parking lot behind the shed rows.

Ashleigh followed her parents, walking slowly as she took in all the activity on the backside of the track. At the end of each shed row was a wash rack. Ashleigh watched grooms hose their charges down and rub shampoo into their coats. Some of the horses put up a fuss, spraying water everywhere, their hooves ringing on the cement floor.

A groom led a gray stallion to one of the mechanical hotwalkers between the shed rows. The horse danced on his toes, fighting to be free as the groom clipped his halter to the walker. As the machine started up, moving like a merry-go-round, the stallion pranced around, kicking and fighting the pull on his halter, trying to get ahead of the walker's mechanical arm. Ashleigh frowned, feeling sorry for the frightened animal. He didn't want to be led by the machine.

"Come on, Ashleigh," her mother called.

Ashleigh whirled around to see her parents well down the row of stalls. She looked back at the gray stallion. He had begun to settle down and was letting the hotwalker set the pace. Relieved to see he was all right, Ashleigh hurried after her parents.

When they reached the stalls where the Danworths had said they'd be stabled, Aladdin and his trainer, Mike Smith, were nowhere in sight. Mr. Griffen paused in front of a stall where a handsome chestnut stallion stood. "This was supposed to be Aladdin's stall," he said.

Ashleigh noticed a dark-haired boy coming up the aisle. He was nice-looking, but when he saw the Griffens, his face darkened into a scowl. "Did you need something?" he asked, and stepped between Mr. Griffen and the horse.

The boy must have been about Caroline's age. Ashleigh's father gazed at him for a moment. "We're looking for the Danworths' horses," he explained.

"This is Townsend Acres' stabling," he said. "I don't know where any Danworth horses are, and I'm not a tour guide for the track."

His tone made Ashleigh bristle. He didn't have to talk to her father that way.

Mr. Griffen eyed the boy for a moment. "Thank you," he said, and turned away. Ashleigh and Mrs. Griffen waited at the end of the shed row while Mr. Griffen went in search of a track official. The boy stayed near the chestnut horse, glaring at them.

"He's rude," Ashleigh said to her mother.

Mrs. Griffen put her arm around Ashleigh's shoulder. "He's just protective of his horse, sweetheart. As I recall, you didn't like Peter Danworth much, either, until you got to know him."

Ashleigh didn't say anything. Peter had been upset about the fact that Aladdin was not racing well, and Ashleigh understood that. But as far as she could tell, this boy just seemed mean and snotty.

Finally Mr. Griffen returned, looking grim.

"There was a mix-up in the stall assignments," he said, and started down another aisle. Ashleigh and her mother followed. "Aladdin is stabled down here."

The row of stalls Mr. Griffen led them down was more closed-in than the other one, facing the back of another shed row. Ashleigh frowned. Aladdin wouldn't like being stuck there, facing a solid wall, with stalls on both sides of him. He liked open spaces, and he liked to see what was going on.

Suddenly Ashleigh heard a rapid banging sound, like blows from a hammer, and then the loud, strident trumpeting of an upset horse. Ashleigh recognized Mike Smith as a stall door was flung open down the aisle. Another loud call rang in Ashleigh's ears, and the sound of hooves kicking against the walls echoed through the air.

"It's Aladdin!" Ashleigh cried. "He going to hurt himself kicking like that!" She broke into a run, darting ahead of her parents and toward the angry stallion's stall.

3

Ashleigh skidded to a stop at the stall door. Her parents were right behind her.

The big black stallion arched his neck and emitted another loud, angry whinny. The whites of Aladdin's eyes flashed as he pinned his ears and kicked at the stall wall. When he dug at the bedding with his front hoof, slamming the stall door with his knee, Ashleigh gasped in horror. Aladdin raised his head and let out another shrill cry.

"No, Aladdin!" Ashleigh called. She stood on her tiptoes, but even stretching her arm as high as she could, she couldn't reach his nose. "You need to settle down," she said firmly.

Mike stood beside Aladdin, stroking the big colt's shoulder, trying to calm the upset animal. When he saw the Griffens, a relieved look crossed his face. "Hey, am I glad to see you guys!"

Aladdin's attention locked on Ashleigh. He tilted his head forward and sniffed at her fingertips. He looked okay, despite his antics. Maybe he just needed some time to settle down, she thought. But Ashleigh's face darkened into a frown when she saw Aladdin's sweat-soaked chest.

"He's going to hurt himself in here," Mike said. "We made it clear we needed an end stall, and we were supposed to have an empty stall next to it. Aladdin doesn't like being closed in like this. I don't know how they got the stalls mixed up, but he's not going to be in any shape to race next week if he's all worked up."

Ashleigh leaned over the half door. Aladdin flared his nostrils and lipped her outstretched hand. "You need to calm down, you big silly," she murmured, tickling his nose with her fingers. "You can't get so upset."

"What did the track officials say?" Mr. Griffen asked Mike.

"I can't get a straight answer," the trainer said, patting Aladdin's dark shoulder.

Ashleigh rubbed Aladdin's upper lip, and the stallion lowered his head more, blowing out his breath tiredly. Mike sighed in relief.

"Good job, Ashleigh," he said. "You're exactly what he needed." He glanced past Ashleigh at her father. "I was just on the phone with Mr. Danworth when I heard Aladdin throwing another fit," he said. "Mr. D. is still trying to get the mix-up straightened out, and my groom got the flu. The poor kid was so sick, I had to send him back to Florida. Fortunately Peter rode up with me for the weekend. I'm going to need all the help I can get."

"Peter's here?" Ashleigh asked excitedly. "Caroline's going to be upset that she didn't come with us after all." But deep down she was glad Caroline had stayed home. When her sister and Peter got together, all they talked about was teenager stuff. Ashleigh liked being with Peter when he wanted to talk about horses.

"He's around here somewhere," Mike said.

Aladdin hung his head over the door, letting Ashleigh rub his forehead. "You're not going to be in very good running form if you keep thrashing around, you dummy."

The colt heaved a sigh and tipped his head so Ashleigh could massage his ear.

Mike stepped away from his shoulder. "Ashleigh, you're hired. That's the calmest I've seen him since we got here. You really do have a way with horses."

Ashleigh glanced up. "Thanks," she said, smiling. "I hope it will help me be a good jockey."

"Oh, it will, don't you worry," Mike assured her. He slipped out of the stall and joined her parents in the aisle.

"Let's go give Mr. Danworth a call while Ashleigh's got Aladdin distracted," Mr. Griffen said. "Maybe there's something I can do to clear up this stall situation."

"I'll stay here with Ashleigh," Mrs. Griffen said. She unfolded a camp stool propped beside the stall and sat down. Ashleigh hung over the stall door, talking to Aladdin all the while.

When Ashleigh's father and Mike returned several minutes later, Peter and a third man had joined them. The stranger was much shorter than her dad and Mike, and had broad shoulders and a lean build. He looked like a jockey, but he walked with a limp and carried a cane with a silver horse head on its handle.

"Hi, Peter," Ashleigh said, smiling at the tall, sandy-haired boy as she continued to rub Aladdin's nose.

"Hey, Ash, how're you doing?" Peter walked up to the stall while the adults talked among themselves. He reached up to scratch Aladdin's neck. "Been on any runaway stallions lately?"

Ashleigh felt her face heat up at the memory of her wild ride on Aladdin.

Peter grinned at her. "It was a good thing we were on the beach when he ran away with you. You really flew when you came off him."

Ashleigh raised her chin and looked Peter square in the eyes. "It was worth falling off if it helped

Aladdin. And it was worth the trouble I got in, too."

"The trouble *we* got in," Peter corrected her. "You'll be amazed to see him run next weekend. He's going great. I'm sure he'll win."

Peter had certainly changed his tune. Before Ashleigh discovered that the shadow roll would work, he had been so convinced Aladdin was a loser he didn't even want to watch him race.

"I can hardly wait," Ashleigh said.

"Ashleigh," Mike said, drawing her attention away from the colt, "I'd like you to meet my friend Sam Wiggins. If you really want to be a jockey, he's the man to talk to. Sam knows more about how to get a horse to run a great race than any other jockey I've ever met."

Ashleigh shook Sam's hand. "Have you won lots of races?"

"Ashleigh, don't be rude," her mother said.

"That's okay." Sam grinned. "It's actually a good question. If someone was going to tell me how to ride a winning race, I'd like to know that he'd won plenty of them himself."

The Griffens, Peter, and Mike began to discuss Aladdin's stall situation, leaving Ashleigh to talk to Sam.

Sam leaned over the stall door to stroke Aladdin's nose. "The answer to your question is yes," he said.

"I've ridden lots of winners, and I've ridden on just about every track from Del Mar to Gulfstream. I rode a lot of small tracks at first, before I worked my way up to riding in the really big races."

Ashleigh eyed the ex-jockey, who was wearing jeans and a black cowboy hat. She tried to imagine him in racing silks.

"But it's hard to ride other horses after you've been on one as great as Secretariat—"

"You rode Secretariat?" Ashleigh interrupted. Now Sam had her complete attention. "That is so cool! Aladdin's sire is Secretariat's full brother. Only Royal Tee never got a chance to run many races."

Sam rubbed Aladdin's silky black nose. "I know," he said, giving her a quick smile. "I was Royal Tee's jockey."

Ashleigh stared at him in amazement. "But he was injured in his fourth race," she protested. "And his jockey was so badly hurt he was never rode again. . . ." Her voice trailed off as her gaze slipped to Sam's cane.

Sam nodded. "Royal was one smart horse, Ashleigh. Just like his brother. He was independent and bossy, but what a ride! When you were on him, you knew you had a great horse under you."

"Like Aladdin," Ashleigh said with a smile, looking at the horse. She glanced back at Sam. "Did you ever get to race Secretariat?"

Sam gave her a sad smile. "I was supposed to ride him in the Bay Shore Stakes at Aqueduct. I like to think I could have taken him all the way to the Preakness. But Royal and I had a race earlier in the day. We got into a crush at the first turn and he went down. We both tore up our legs pretty good. Now I breed winners instead of riding them," he explained.

"Do you miss racing?"

Sam nodded. "Of course I do. I love racing. But being a jockey is a dangerous job, Ashleigh."

"I know," she said. "But that's what I want to do. I'm going to be the best jockey ever."

Sam looked at her hard. "It takes guts and skill and a lot of determination."

Aladdin nudged her, trying to rub against her shoulder. Ashleigh reached up and scratched his dark forehead. He shifted his weight, making it clear he wanted his neck rubbed as well.

Sam continued to talk about his racing past, and Ashleigh listened, leaning into Aladdin's stall, rubbing as much of the colt's head and neck as she could reach.

"Well, he looks pretty content." At the sound of Mike's voice, Ashleigh and Sam turned around.

Peter grinned at her. "Hey, Mike," he said, "if you don't want to take Aladdin to Edgardale while they get the stall business right, maybe Ashleigh could just stay here to keep him calm."

"What? We're taking Aladdin home?" Ashleigh couldn't believe her ears.

Her father nodded. "We can put him in the big broodmare stall at the far end of the barn, with Moe across the aisle for company. He'll be better off there until this mess is straightened out. We can't leave him here. Not like this."

"What about his track work?" Ashleigh demanded. She would love to have Aladdin at home, even if just for a little while. But he needed to have a track to train on.

"We've got that taken care of," Mike said. "Do you know where Shady Valley Farm is?"

Ashleigh nodded. Shady Valley was a training farm not too far from Edgardale.

"I used to work with some of their horses," Mike said. "They said we could use their training track to work Aladdin while he's at Edgardale."

"Did you hear that, boy?" Ashleigh turned back to the stallion. "You get to come home!"

"It'll be a while before I'm ready to load him in the trailer," Mike said. "I'll get him to Edgardale as soon as I get everything taken care of here."

"Elaine and I can give you a hand," Mr. Griffen offered.

"I'd appreciate the help," Mike said. "We can get it done much quicker."

"Can I go watch a couple of races, then?" Ashleigh asked. She couldn't pass up a chance like this. If it were up to her, she'd be at the track every day.

"Why don't you go with her, Peter?" Mike said.

"Sure," Peter said. "Let's go, Ashleigh."

They found places along the rail in time to watch the post parade go by.

"I'll take the number two horse," Peter said, indicating a prancing gray.

"There's my horse," Ashleigh said, pointing at a black stallion with the number five on his blanket.

As the Thoroughbreds circled the track with the pony horses, Ashleigh grew tense, anticipating the moment when she would feel the ground rumbling as the racing horses flew past. She loved the sound of pounding hooves, the whoosh of the wind the speeding horses created, the rhythmic puffing of their breath.

"Sam was really impressed when Mike told him how you figured out that Aladdin needed the shadow roll," Peter told her, leaning his elbows on the rail.

"Sam's really a nice guy," Ashleigh commented, watching as the horses neared the starting gate.

"My dad and Mike say the racing world lost a great jockey when he had to retire," Peter said. "Mike says you can tell which jockeys Sam's been coaching. They get the best from their horses. He could really teach you a lot, Ashleigh."

"Why would a famous jockey care about me?" Ashleigh asked. "I'm still way too young to be a jockey."

Peter made a face. "But you'll never be too big," he said. Peter was Aladdin's owner and primary exercise rider, but he was already too tall ever to be a jockey. He looked away as the last horse was loaded into the starting gate.

Ashleigh gripped the rail when the gates flew open. She leaned forward as the horses exploded across the starting line and shot past them in a thundering blur of legs. Ashleigh stretched over the rail, keeping an eye on her favorite. For a while he was near the front of the pack, but as the race continued he dropped back. When they crossed the finish line, her horse was in third.

"His jockey shouldn't have pushed him so hard," she said to Peter as they headed back toward the shed rows. "He would have been better off getting a feel for the pace before he took the lead."

"At least your horse placed," Peter scoffed good-naturedly. "Number two looked like he was asleep!"

When they reached the parking lot, Ashleigh's parents had everything loaded in the trailer except Aladdin.

"I'm going to see if Mike needs a hand," Peter said, heading back to the shed row. "See you soon."

"Where's Aladdin?" Ashleigh asked.

"We need to hurry home and get his stall ready," Mrs. Griffen said. "Mike is taking care of some paperwork, and then he and Peter will drive Aladdin over to the farm."

When they pulled up to the house, Ashleigh hopped from the car and hurried over to the house to change into her riding clothes. She couldn't wait to get on Stardust and practice some of the moves she had just seen the jockeys use to gallop their horses.

Rory and Caroline met her at the door.

"You gotta watch this, Ash!" Rory was holding a windup car in each hand as he jumped up and down, waving his arms.

Ashleigh sighed impatiently. "What is it?"

"Mom, Dad, watch!"

Mr. and Mrs. Griffen paused in the doorway. "What are you doing with the fan?"

It wasn't until Mrs. Griffen spoke that Ashleigh saw the big fan they used during the summer, sitting in the middle of the hallway.

"This!" Rory held out his cars, and Ashleigh saw that he and Caroline had taped a stick with a piece of paper to the top of one, making a sail of sorts. Rory wound both cars up and aimed them toward the fan.

"Ready, Rory?" Caroline put her hand on the fan's switch.

"Go!" At his command, Caroline turned the fan on and Rory released the cars. Ashleigh and her parents watched while the car with the sail caught the wind and went off course, crashing into the wall. The other car kept a straight course until it unwound and stopped in front of the fan.

"It's something with wind," Rory explained. "I can't remember the word."

"Resistance," Caroline finished. "Wind resistance, remember?"

"We watched *The Crazy Scientist Show* on TV this afternoon," Rory said. "He does fun stuff."

Ashleigh eyed the cars, then the fan, then threw her arms around her brother. "Thank you, Rory!" She laughed. "Thanks tons and tons."

Rory looked confused. "What did I do?"

"You're just a great brother, that's all." Ashleigh scrambled up the stairs. Her science project dilemma was solved. She would borrow Rory's cars and take a blow-dryer to school instead of the fan. Wind resistance. She grinned to herself. She had her project for the science fair.

The phone rang as she came downstairs.

"Ash, it's Mona," Caroline called.

Ashleigh hurried into the kitchen and picked up the receiver. "Guess what? Aladdin's coming to Edgardale!"

"Ooh, I can't wait to see him," Mona said. "Hey, Ash, I had a great time at the show."

"How'd you and Frisky do?" Ashleigh felt a twinge of guilt. She had almost forgotten about Mona's show.

"I'll tell you when you come over," Mona said, sounding giddy. "I have something to show you. How soon can you get here?"

"As soon as I get Stardust tacked up." Ashleigh hung up and hurried to the barn, where her parents were working on Aladdin's stall.

"Is it okay if I to go over to Mona's?" she asked.

"But don't you want to be here when Aladdin arrives?" Mrs. Griffen asked.

Ashleigh paused. Of course she did. But she wanted to ride with Mona, too. "I won't be gone very long," she promised.

"Okay, then," her mother said. "Have fun."

In minutes she had Stardust out of her paddock, saddled, and ready to go. She urged the mare into a fast walk down the drive, then trotted her beside the road and up the Gardeners' driveway.

Mona stood in front of the barn, waving her arms. She had changed from her show clothes and was wearing jeans and a sweatshirt, just like Ashleigh.

Ashleigh stopped Stardust. "Where's Frisky? Aren't we going to ride?"

"In a minute," Mona said. "I have to show you something."

Ashleigh swung out of the saddle and followed Mona into the barn. From her stall Frisky whinnied, and Stardust answered. The girls laughed. "Do you think they ask each other how their humans are?" Mona asked, leading the way to Frisky's stall.

She pointed at the door, where three ribbons hung in a row.

"You got two blues!" Ashleigh eyed the gold print on the rosettes, which showed the outline of a horse and rider going over a jump. "That is so cool."

A bit of wind fluttered the ribbons. Stardust snorted and angled her head to eye them. Ashleigh stroked the mare's neck and swallowed a pang of envy. It was going to be a long time until she could be a jockey. Mona would have Frisky's stall covered with ribbons before Ashleigh even got to exercise-ride a Thoroughbred.

"I got the white one in equitation on the flat," Mona said with a shrug. "I still need to work on my form, but fourth place isn't so bad. You should have seen us go over those jumps, Ash. Frisky was great."

"Were the jumps really hard?"

Mona laughed. "No way! They were fun. They had one with stripes like a circus tent. Two of the horses refused it, but Frisky went right over. The best jump looked like a pile of tangled-up branches. But it was easy. You could have done that course with Stardust, Ashleigh. No problem."

Ashleigh thought about going around the arena alone, all eyes on her as she jumped. She shook her head. "Not a chance. Not all by myself. I'd be so nervous I'd fall off while Stardust was standing still!"

Mona's eyed widened and a grin broke across her face. "But what if we rode together?"

"What do you mean?" Ashleigh frowned at her friend.

"Pairs jumping. We'd do just what we've been practicing. Frisky and Stardust are perfect together. And there's a pairs class at tomorrow's show."

"No way!" Ashleigh exclaimed. "I've never even taken lessons or anything. I'm not good enough to show."

"We can practice right now," Mona pressed her.

"But Aladdin's coming today," Ashleigh said. "I need to help him settle in."

"Your parents and Jonas are there. Come on, Ashleigh. It'll be great. And we won't be gone very long tomorrow, anyway."

Ashleigh bit her lower lip. Mike and her parents really didn't need her help with Aladdin, and it would be fun to show with Mona. Maybe they'd even win a ribbon!

"Okay," she agreed finally. "Go and get Frisky and let's practice jumping together."

4

By the time Ashleigh rode home the lights were on in the barn. A large silver horse van was parked near the barn door. Compared to the Griffens' trailer, the Danworths' horse van was huge.

Quickly Ashleigh untacked Stardust and put her away before hurrying down to where everyone was gathered in front of Aladdin's stall. Moe looked content in the stall across the aisle.

"Look, Ashleigh," Rory said. "Moe gets to be an important horse."

Ashleigh smiled. "Moe's always important." She rubbed the pony's shaggy forelock.

Aladdin was eating a flake of hay, looking very relaxed in his new quarters.

"I think he's happy," Mike said, smiling at Ashleigh.

She gave the stallion's nose a stroke. "He likes being here, don't you, fellow?"

Her parents stood back a bit, gazing at the big black racehorse.

"Well, he was born here. Can you believe he was one of our foals?" Mr. Griffen sighed. "They grow up so fast."

"Don't start getting sentimental, Derek," Ashleigh's mother said in a teasing voice.

Ashleigh glanced around. "Where's Peter?" she asked.

"He and Caroline went up to the house," her mother said. "Peter is going to spend the night in Rory's room. He has to fly back to Florida tomorrow afternoon so he can go to school on Monday, just like you."

"Come on, Ashleigh, Rory. Let's leave Aladdin alone for the night. Mike will be here to take care of him," her father said, turning away.

Ashleigh wanted to protest. She hadn't had a chance to spend any time with Aladdin. But it was her own fault—she had chosen to go riding with Mona instead of being there when Aladdin arrived. The next morning she would get up extra early so she could groom Aladdin—and Stardust, she reminded herself. But first she had to ask her parents if she could take Stardust to the show.

Mrs. Griffen invited Mike to dinner, but he and Jonas turned out to be old track acquaintances, and they decided to spend the evening swapping stories.

"I have everything I need in the horse van," Mike said. "Those living quarters are as nice as a regular apartment."

So, after saying good night, the Griffens headed for the house.

Ashleigh fell into step beside her parents. "Mom, Dad, can I take Stardust to a schooling show tomorrow?"

Her mother looked at her in surprise. "What kind of show?"

"Pairs jumping with Mona," Ashleigh said, walking up onto the porch. "Mrs. Gardener will trailer the horses for us, and the entry fee for the class is only a few dollars."

"Jumping?" Her father raised his eyebrows. "What happened to the world's greatest jockey?"

Ashleigh sighed. "I still want to be a jockey, but I'm too young to race right now. I thought I could take Stardust to some little shows. It'll be fun to ride with Mona and everything."

Mr. and Mrs. Griffen exchanged a look. Ashleigh's eyes darted from one to the other. She didn't know how her parents communicated without talking, but they seemed to have a secret language.

Finally Mrs. Griffen looked at Ashleigh and nodded. "That's fine, if you want to spend the rest of your allowance this week on entry fees," she said.

"Great!" Ashleigh said.

After dinner Peter disappeared into the living room
with Rory and Caroline to play a board game. It was
Ashleigh's turn to do the dishes. She finished them
quickly, then called Mona to tell her the good news.
When she finally got off the phone, she headed
upstairs to go through her closet. Mona had told her
she should wear a ratcatcher shirt, along with jodhpurs and a riding jacket, but Ashleigh knew she didn't
have any of the right clothes. She opened the closet
door, staring at the rumpled clothes on her side of the
closet. She had nothing even remotely suitable.

"What's this?" Caroline asked, coming into the
room. "Ashleigh the grunge princess is having a fashion crisis?"

Ashleigh looked over her shoulder at her sister. "I
need riding breeches and a jacket," she said desperately. "And I don't even have the right kind of shirt."

"I thought jockeys wore silks," Caroline said, sitting
down on her bed.

"I'm going to ride with Mona at a show tomorrow,"
Ashleigh said, leaning against the closet door.

Caroline started to open her mouth, then clamped

her lips shut. Ashleigh sighed in relief. She didn't need Caroline teasing her about clothes just then.

But Caroline rose and stepped around Ashleigh, reaching into her own side of the closet. She pulled out a hanger with a pair of beige jodhpurs draped over it. "Mom bought these for me a couple of years ago. She thought nice riding clothes might get me more interested in horses." Caroline rolled her eyes. "It didn't work. I wasn't as short as you are, but if you're wearing tall boots, it won't matter." She offered the pants to Ashleigh and turned back to the closet. "I don't have a show shirt," she said. "But here's a white turtleneck. I think that'll work. And maybe Mom has a jacket."

"Thanks, Caro. You're a lifesaver," Ashleigh said gratefully.

"I know," her sister said. "Now, do you want to play some cards with Peter and Rory and me?"

"Sure," Ashleigh said and followed her sister downstairs.

Ashleigh was disappointed when she went to the barn early Sunday morning. Mike and Peter had already taken Aladdin to Shady Valley for his workout. If only she'd been a little earlier, she could have gone with them. But it was a good thing she'd stayed home. It was taking forever to turn Stardust into a show horse.

"This has got to be the stupidest thing to do to a horse's mane," Ashleigh exclaimed, exasperated, as she stood on an overturned crate next to her mare, weaving a clump of mane into a crooked braid. Stardust bobbed her head, jerking the braid from Ashleigh's hand.

"Knock it off!" Ashleigh put her hands on her hips and glared at the mare. "You're supposed to have all these dumb little braids. Then after the show we have to take them all out. It makes no sense." She liked the horses better with their manes flowing free. You never saw a racehorse with its mane all tied up. But Mona had explained that the horses in hunter classes were supposed to have braided manes.

"Move over."

At the sound of Caroline's voice, Ashleigh looked over her shoulder. Her sister stood at Stardust's head.

"Don't just stare at me, Ash. Move."

Ashleigh jumped down, and Caroline climbed onto the crate.

"You go wrap her tail. I'll do the mane." She held out her hand, and Ashleigh dropped a comb and a fat plastic needle strung with brown yarn onto her palm.

Ashleigh began to work on Stardust's tail and eyed her sister over the mare's round rump. "Thanks, Caro.

I know you don't like horses very much, but I'm not good at braiding."

Caroline picked up a piece of mane and quickly formed it into a smooth braid, using the needle and yarn to tack it up. "It isn't that I don't like the horses. I just don't eat, sleep, and breathe them like the rest of you. Sometimes I feel like I got born into the wrong family."

Ashleigh frowned. She'd never thought about how Caroline felt being the only person in the family who wasn't horse-crazy. Ashleigh wondered how she would feel if she were the only one in the family who cared about horses.

"Do you think we're all nuts?" she asked, working the roll of wrap around the base of Stardust's tail.

Caroline laughed, her nimble fingers forming braid after braid down Stardust's sleek neck, rolling them under, and fastening them with the yarn. "No, Ash. I don't think you're nuts. I just think there are lots of other interesting things in life besides horses. If that was all anyone cared about, the world wouldn't be anything but horses." She shuddered. "Hay and manure as far as the eye could see."

Ashleigh thought about it for a minute. "No clothing stores in the mall, just tack shops. No regular school, just riding lessons." A grin split her face. The world would be a perfect place, she decided. But she kept her thoughts to herself.

When Caroline was done, the girls stood back to admire Stardust. The mare arched her neck and swung her head around. The braids stayed neatly in place. Stardust looked as good as any of the horses Ashleigh had seen in show magazines.

"She's beautiful," Ashleigh breathed.

"You're welcome," Caroline said, smiling.

"Thanks, Caro." Ashleigh giggled. "You know, sometimes you're an okay sister."

"I know." Caroline started down the barn aisle, then stopped and glanced back at Ashleigh. "Do good at the show, all right?"

"I will," Ashleigh promised.

When the Gardeners' truck pulled up by the barn, Ashleigh quickly slipped Stardust's nylon blanket on and unclipped the mare from the crossties.

Her parents met her in the barn doorway.

"We dug around in the closet and I found this old riding jacket. It's big, but it'll do the trick," Mrs. Griffen said.

She took Stardust's lead as Ashleigh tried on the blue wool jacket. The sleeves were too long and it was big and boxy, but it was wearable.

Ashleigh buttoned the jacket and straightened the collar of her white turtleneck. "How do I look?" she asked with a giggle.

"Very proper," her father said, smiling approvingly.

"I wish we could see you at your first show, Ashleigh," her mother said, "but we have some clients coming today to look at this year's foal crop."

Ashleigh wished breeders wouldn't refer to the foals as a crop, even though it was a common term. It made the colts and fillies seem like nothing more than tomatoes or wheat, something to be harvested. When she owned her own breeding and training farm she would never call her foals a crop.

"It's okay." Ashleigh gave them a bright smile. Secretly she was glad they wouldn't be there. She wanted to feel a little more sure of herself before they watched her ride in a show.

"Well," her father said, "have a good time."

"I will. I have to go. Mrs. Gardener is waiting for us."

Ashleigh led Stardust into the trailer and tied her beside Frisky.

"We're going to be fine, Stardust," she whispered to the horse. Stardust looked relaxed and very professional in her neat braids and nylon sheet, but on the ride to the show Ashleigh's stomach felt as though a dozen butterflies had taken up residence there. *It's just a few easy jumps,* she told herself. *And Mona will be right beside me.*

When they pulled into the show grounds, Ashleigh looked out the truck window, curiously taking in all the sights. Mrs. Gardener parked beside a blue truck and matching trailer. Everywhere Ashleigh looked she saw riders dressed in light breeches and dark jackets, and horses with braided manes and glistening coats.

"Isn't this great?" Mona called as she hopped from the truck. Ashleigh followed slowly, looking around. To her relief, none of the horses looked any more spectacular than Stardust. Stardust loved to jump, and Ashleigh knew she was a good rider, so she decided to relax.

She tried to see if she recognized anyone. Jamie and Lynne wouldn't be there. Lynne's father was calling races at Churchill Downs, so Lynne had gone to Louisville that day. And Jamie was home with a cold.

Ashleigh noticed a small group of girls gathered near a shiny white truck and trailer. They had their heads together, laughing and talking. They looked about Ashleigh and Mona's age, but they were obviously not newcomers to the world of horse shows. Their hair was neatly done up in buns, and their clothes fitted perfectly. The sun caught the polished leather of their tall boots. One had the chin strap of her black velvet helmet dangling from her fingertips.

Ashleigh glanced down at her own ill-fitting jodhpurs and scuffed riding boots. Her mother's old riding jacket was really loose and too long.

She brought her hand up to feel her own hastily

pinned hair and grimaced. Pieces were already coming undone. She should have asked Caroline to braid it. Suddenly Ashleigh wished she had stayed home. She could have ridden Stardust over to Shady Valley to watch Peter ride Aladdin on the track.

"Here's a hairnet, Ashleigh," Mrs. Gardener said, coming up behind her. "No one is going to see your hair under the helmet. This will keep it nicely out of the way."

Ashleigh flashed her a grateful smile. "Thanks," she said.

Mona came back from the registration table with their numbers and a schedule. "I'm going to jump in the twelve-and-under class, then we're number three in the pairs competition," she told Ashleigh. "After that I have my equitation class, and then we're done."

Mona and Ashleigh got their horses from the trailer. Ashleigh busied herself tacking up Stardust. Her all-purpose saddle was old, but she took good care of it. The worn leather gleamed softly from the many polishings she had given it.

Ashleigh could hear some of the other riders calling to each other as they saddled their horses. Some girls she didn't know greeted Mona, who called back cheerfully. Ashleigh began to feel a little lonely. She didn't know the people Mona knew from her jumping lessons. She didn't have a special saddle for jumping.

She didn't have the right clothes, and now she didn't feel very sure of herself. She was out of place.

"I can't do this, Mona," she said quietly. "I don't belong here."

"What?" Mona peeked under Frisky's neck and stared hard at her. "Of course you can do it, Ash. I'll be right beside you. Come and see what we'll be jumping."

She followed Mona to the jumping course. It was very much like the course Mona's father had set up in the Gardeners' paddock, only the jumps were a little fancier, with gleaming white poles and brightly painted standards supporting them. One of the jumps had flower boxes bursting with colorful plants at each end, and one had potted trees beside the standards. But none of the jumps was any higher than what they'd been jumping at Mona's.

Ashleigh turned to smile at her friend. "You're right, Mona. We'll be fine," she said.

They hurried back to get their horses. Mrs. Gardener had trimmed the corners of their cardboard competitors' numbers so they would fit better on their backs. She pinned Mona's number to the back of her jacket.

"How do I look?" Mona craned her neck, trying to see the number.

"It's even," Ashleigh said, and turned around so

Mrs. Gardener could put on her number.

"Yours looks good, too," Mona said when her mother was done. The girls swung up onto their horses and rode into the practice arena to warm up. As they jogged Frisky and Stardust side-by-side Ashleigh noticed the same group of well-dressed girls on their horses. Aside from their perfect clothes and polished tack, their riding didn't look any better than Mona's. And Ashleigh was sure she rode just as well as Mona did.

She and Mona trotted past two of the girls. One was on a pretty gray mare, but the other girl's horse was the one that caught Ashleigh's eye. He was a black gelding and, judging by his conformation, a well-bred Thoroughbred. With his long neck and powerful hindquarters, he looked like a racehorse. Ashleigh was tempted to ask the girl about his bloodlines.

Then the girl on the gray said loudly, "Look, Danielle. That one got her riding clothes out of the rag-bag." Ashleigh felt her back stiffen. She knew they were talking about her. Her face felt hot and she gritted her teeth, determined not to wheel around and say something rude.

"It's a good thing this is a schooling show, not a fashion show," the other girl said.

Ashleigh wanted to turn around and tell them off, but instead she kept riding.

She heard the first girl snort. "You'd think she'd put some effort into her appearance anyway."

"Forget about her, Debbie. We need to practice."

Ashleigh felt her stomach drop. Great. They were riding in the pairs class, too! Mona shot her a reassuring glance. "Just ignore them, Ash. Some of these girls don't realize how lucky they are to have a horse in the first place," she said. "Come on, let's canter over that rail at the end."

They picked up the canter, their horses perfectly in sync, and popped easily over the rail, landing together.

"Perfect!" Mona cried. "If we can do that in there, we're set!" But as she spoke, Ashleigh had to pull Stardust up short to keep from careening into Debbie's horse as she and Danielle jumped a cross rail in the other direction.

Ashleigh tried to keep from getting frazzled, but the practice ring had such a competitive air, it was hard to keep her nerves at bay. She looked at Mona. Her best friend was beaming as she watched the other riders on their horses. She seemed to be in her element.

Finally the loudspeaker whined. The announcer cleared his throat and called for the first class.

A girl on a stocky Appaloosa rode onto the course. She cantered the gelding around the ring once, then headed him for the first fence.

Ashleigh watched their approach closely. The rider kept pulling on the reins, and her mount seemed confused by the cues he was getting from her busy hands. Ashleigh winced, waiting for the sound of hooves striking the wooden rail. But the horse popped over the obstacle and landed hard, throwing the girl onto his shoulders. He headed for the next jump as she regained her seat. They made it over the second jump, but Ashleigh felt her own tension grow as the horse clipped the third rail and sent it rolling. When the girl rode out of the ring, she looked ready to cry.

Ashleigh felt bad for her. *I hope I don't mess up when we go,* she thought. Then the next rider entered. It was the blond girl on the black gelding. She circled the ring at a canter and headed for the first jump. The gelding took off nicely and flew over the jump with plenty of room to spare. His landing was light, and the girl sat down and turned him for the next jump. They cleared all the jumps and rode from the ring, the girl sitting tall in the saddle. Their round looked perfect, as far as Ashleigh could tell.

The third horse knocked down the second rail, but the fourth horse had a clean round. Ashleigh felt her stomach drop even lower. Some of them made it look impossible, and some looked as though they could jump the course in their sleep.

When Mona rode onto the course she looked as if

she was having the time of her life. She and Frisky circled the ring, then turned to approach the first jump. Ashleigh kept her fists clenched and held her breath, releasing it in a gust when Mona and Frisky sailed over the first jump with practiced ease. Ashleigh relaxed her hands. Mona and Frisky completed the course with a clean round, and Ashleigh applauded as they left the ring.

When the judge called the riders back in for ribbons, Mona and Frisky took second, and the blond girl got the blue.

Mona joined Ashleigh and Stardust to wait for their turn in the pairs class. They watched the first two sets of riders complete the course. The first riders, the girls on the black gelding and the gray mare, cleared all the jumps, but they didn't stay in step. When the second pair rode, one of the horses clipped a rail, sending it clattering to the ground.

When Ashleigh and Mona rode into the ring, Ashleigh felt as though the entire world had stopped. She glanced at Mona, who gave her a confident smile. "We're on the best two horses here, right?"

"Right," Ashleigh agreed.

They cantered their horses around the ring, then headed for the first jump. Frisky and Stardust were in perfect harmony when they sailed over the fence, and Ashleigh felt her tension ease. She focused on taking

Stardust through the course in rhythm with Frisky's strides. They sailed over each obstacle, then turned in stride and cantered to the next. When they finished with a clean round, the two horses were still in step. Ashleigh rode from the ring, smiling and patting Stardust's shoulder as she gasped for breath. She'd been so nervous, she'd forgotten to breathe!

Ashleigh stopped Stardust outside the ring and glanced at Mona.

"We did it, Ash," Mona said, hugging Frisky around the neck. "We had a perfect round!"

The competitors lined their horses up outside the ring, waiting for the judge's final decision. A few minutes of tense silence passed while the judge handed his notes to the ring steward. Stardust shifted impatiently. A baby began to cry in the stands. Then the sound system crackled and the announcer called, "We now have the results of the pairs jumping. In first place . . ."

When Ashleigh heard Mona's name, followed by her own, she could hardly believe it. Mona gasped and walked Frisky into the ring. Stardust followed automatically, and Ashleigh felt a thrill down to her boots when the judge clipped a blue ribbon on Frisky's headstall and a second one on Stardust's bridle. Her face flushed with pride. They'd won—her first blue ribbon!

The last classes of the day passed in a happy blur. Ashleigh cheered Mona on during her flat class. Mona rode very well, but her canter-to-walk transition was a little messy. Ashleigh watched as the judge awarded ribbons to the best six. Mona took third place, a yellow ribbon. Ashleigh leaned against the rail, silently wishing that she had entered the class, too. *Maybe Mom will get me a nice ratcatcher and a good pair of breeches for my birthday,* she thought.

"That was beginner's luck in the pairs class." A nasty voice behind her interrupted Ashleigh's thoughts. She whirled around to see the girl on the gray mare glaring at her.

The other girl stood nearby, holding the black gelding. Ashleigh still wanted to ask about the horse's bloodlines, but she couldn't let the other girl's comment slide.

"This may be my first show," she said, "but I'm not a beginner. And it wasn't luck. Mona and I practiced hard."

The girl with the black gelding put her hand on the other girl's arm. "We just need more practice, Debbie," she said. "There are a lot more shows this spring, and I plan on riding in all of them. We'll get another chance."

But Debbie scowled at Ashleigh. "I still think it was luck," she said.

"I'll show you just how lucky I am next time," Ashleigh said, and instantly regretted her words. She didn't even know when the next schooling show was, or if her parents would let her go.

"See you Wednesday at Bluefield Farm, then," Debbie said, looking smug.

"Come on," Danielle said. "We need to get the horses ready to go. My dad is waiting."

Ashleigh sighed with relief when they walked away. She hurried to the Gardeners' trailer, where Mona was busy untacking Frisky.

"That was so great, Mona," she said breathlessly. "Do you think you're going to the Bluefield Farm show, too?"

"I think so," Mona said, spinning around to look at Ashleigh. "Wow, do you want to go? Oh, Ash, that would be so great."

"I really want to," Ashleigh said. "But this time I want to ride in the equitation class, too. We have to show those girls we can win, even if I don't have the right clothes and stuff."

"That's right. And we're going to have a blast showing," Mona promised. "This is just the beginning."

As they drove home, Mona chattered excitedly about all the shows they could enter together. But as they passed a training stable Ashleigh saw an exercise rider breezing a black Thoroughbred around the track, and any thought of horse shows was pushed to the back of her mind. In all her excitement at the show, she'd forgotten all about Aladdin. Now she could hardly wait to get home and see him.

5

Mona got Ashleigh's tack from the trailer while Ashleigh put Stardust away.

"Don't forget to ask your parents about the Blue-field show," Mona said, handing Ashleigh her saddle. "Maybe you could start taking lessons with me and Jamie and Lynne, too. That would be so cool."

"I'll ask," Ashleigh promised.

Mona climbed into the cab of the truck. "See you tomorrow," she said, waving out the window.

"Bye. Thanks, Mrs. Gardener," Ashleigh called as Mona's mom waved good-bye, too.

She put her saddle away and gave Stardust a flake of hay. "You were so good today," she said, giving the mare a pat before she hurried down to the other end of the barn. Aladdin and Moe were dozing in their stalls. Aladdin looked up and nickered when Ashleigh stopped in front of him. She pulled at his black forelock.

"Tomorrow," she told him, "I'm going to get up really early so I can see you work at the track." He snuffled at her hands, blowing soft puffs of air onto them. Ashleigh planted a kiss on his black nose, then hurried to the house, where she found her parents in their office.

Her father looked up from the computer screen when Ashleigh held up her blue ribbon. "Very impressive," he said. "We're proud of you, Ash."

"Can I go to another show on Wednesday afternoon?" Ashleigh asked hopefully. "I still have enough money to cover the entry fees."

"How are things going in your math class?" her mother asked.

"Good," Ashleigh said firmly. "I got a B on the quiz we had Friday."

"Then I suppose it would be okay, if Mona's mother is willing to trailer Stardust for you again," Mrs. Griffen said. "We'll make sure we're there to watch you this time. We don't want to miss seeing you show."

"That would be great," Ashleigh said. It would be fun to win another blue ribbon while her parents were there.

"Just remember," her mother added, "you have responsibilities here, too."

"I know." Ashleigh hesitated, then spoke quickly. "Do you think we could put up some practice jumps?" If she was able to do some of her practicing at home, she'd be able to spend more time around Aladdin. "Not anything fancy," she added before they could reply. "Just a couple of rails in one of the empty paddocks. And maybe I could take some jumping lessons, too? Mona, Lynne, and Jamie all love their trainer. The class sounds like a lot of fun."

Her parents looked at each other in another one of their wordless conversations. Ashleigh watched them closely.

Finally Mr. Griffen turned to her. "We can set up a few jumps, but it's going to have to wait until after next week. The Danworths will be here in a few days, and we do have Aladdin on the grounds, so things are a little hectic right now. But after the race next Sunday things will calm down and we can figure out what you need. We can talk more about jumping lessons then, okay?"

Ashleigh nodded. "Thanks," she said, turning for the stairs. "I'm going to go change."

Ashleigh peeled off her riding clothes slowly. She felt torn. She didn't want to miss out on anything to do with Aladdin's training while he was there at Edgardale, but she still wanted to ride with Mona, too. She'd just have to start getting up really early every morning to go to the training track with Mike and Aladdin. Then she could work with Mona on jumping in the afternoons.

When she returned to the barn, she hung the blue ribbon on Stardust's stall and gave the mare a carrot. Stardust looked content, sleepily munching her hay. Ashleigh watched her for a while and then walked down the aisle to visit Aladdin and Moe.

"Hey there, guys." She fed each of them a chunk of carrot, rubbing Moe's shaggy forehead and tickling Aladdin's nose with her fingers. She laughed when he twitched his upper lip back and forth against her fingertips.

Mike came in, pushing an empty wheelbarrow. He put the pitchfork away and parked the cart, then came over to Aladdin's stall.

"Where's Peter?" Ashleigh asked, looking around the quiet barn.

"Jonas drove him up to the airport. Rory and Caroline went along for the ride."

Ashleigh tried not to show her disappointment. She'd barely seen Peter at all. She could have stayed home and spent the day hanging out with Peter and Aladdin, but she'd chosen to go to the show with Mona instead. "How did Aladdin do this morning?" she asked.

"He took to the Shady Valley track like a fish to

water," Mike said. "Peter breezed him today, and we'll have one of the apprentice jockeys Sam has been working with exercise him for the next couple of days. Peter's going to fly back up on Thursday afternoon, though. Aladdin seems to work best for him, and we want the colt in top form for Sunday's race."

Ashleigh frowned. Suddenly her blue ribbon didn't seem so special. She was missing out on all the important things that happened before a horse was ready to step onto the track. Things that she cared about a whole lot more than jumping at some horse show.

Mike smiled at her as though he knew what she was thinking. "I see you and Stardust did okay today," he said, pointing at the blue ribbon fluttering on Stardust's stall. "Pretty soon you'll have all kinds of ribbons to hang on her stall."

Ashleigh shrugged, rubbing Aladdin's gleaming black neck. "It was only the pairs class at a schooling show," she said. "No big deal."

Mike shook his head. "But it was your first show, right?"

"Well, yeah." Aladdin nudged her with his nose, and Ashleigh scratched his chin gently.

"Then you're doing great," Mike said. "Not too many riders get ribbons at their first show, let alone first place. You are well on your way to becoming a great all-around horsewoman, Ashleigh."

Ashleigh smiled up at him, feeling better.

But after she and Caroline had gone to bed that night, Ashleigh tossed and turned, unable to go to sleep. Her mind kept jumping back and forth from the thrill of getting the blue ribbon at the show to how she had missed the chance to watch Aladdin work. She sighed heavily and thumped her pillow, trying to find a comfortable position. Finally she nestled under her blankets with a flashlight and her diary.

Dear Diary,

So much is going on, you won't believe it! Yesterday Aladdin came to Edgardale. He's going to be racing at Keeneland next week. And today I rode Stardust in our first horse show. We did a pairs jumping class with Mona and Frisky, and we got first place! Our first blue ribbon! But one of the other girls said it was beginner's luck. I'll show her! We're going to ride in another show this week. I want Stardust to have so many ribbons on her stall door that the wood won't even show through. I can hardly wait until Wednesday. Mona and I need to practice for the show, but I don't want to miss out on Aladdin's training, either. His trainer, Mike, is so nice and so is his friend Sam, who's an ex-

*jockey. I like talking to them. They always teach
me things. I just don't know what to do.*

It was still dark when Ashleigh's alarm went off on
Monday morning. Caroline didn't even budge when
Ashleigh turned on her bedside lamp. She slipped
into her jeans and a sweatshirt and carried her boots
downstairs. As she hurried out to the barn she could
see lights on in Jonas's apartment in the barn loft. But
Mike was nowhere to be seen, and Aladdin's stall was
empty. She'd missed them.

Stardust called to her, and Ashleigh walked to her
mare's stall to give her a pet. The light in the barn
office was on, and Ashleigh could hear her parents'
voices, but she didn't disturb them. Instead, she hurried back to the house.

The sun was coming up, spreading daylight across
the farm. Ashleigh's bike was parked in the utility
shed, beside Caroline's and Rory's. She clipped on her
bike helmet and hopped on her bike, pedaling as fast
as she could down the driveway. Shady Valley was
only a couple of farms away.

She coasted down the paved drive to the training
farm. A light fog hung over the track. She could see
Mike standing with Sam near the gap in the rail. On

the far side of the track she could see Aladdin jogging, the exercise rider bobbing in time to his huge stride. She parked her bike well away from the track and walked over to Mike and Sam.

Mike gave her a surprised look, but Sam just smiled.

"Did I miss anything?" she asked breathlessly.

"No," Mike said. "The rider just mounted up and started jogging him."

Ashleigh watched in silence, absorbing everything Mike and Sam said about the horse and the rider.

"Relax your hands a bit there," Sam called to the girl on Aladdin's back. "Put your weight back just a little and drop your shoulders. This isn't a race."

Ashleigh wished she could take Aladdin around the oval herself, but then she thought of how she'd lost control when she rode him on the beach. Mike would never let her get back on him.

Aladdin and his rider jogged past the gap, traveling clockwise on the track. The rhythmic tattoo of his hooves on the track and the deep huffing of his breaths filled Ashleigh's ears. The light fog rising above the track and the new sun shimmering over damp Kentucky bluegrass was breathtaking. Ashleigh ached to be the one working a Thoroughbred on the quiet track at the break of day. The girl on Aladdin's back was lucky.

"Ask him to pick up a little speed," Mike called to the jockey.

The girl leaned forward a little and collected the reins. "That's a good start," Mike called. "Now take up a bit more rein."

"Why do you want her to pull back on the reins?" Ashleigh asked, frowning.

Sam flashed her a smile. "She's helping Aladdin by putting some pressure on his mouth. He braces himself against the bit while he's running. It's up to his jockey to give him something to balance against. A horse doesn't win a race by itself, you know."

"But you have to have a really fast horse to do well," Ashleigh countered.

Sam nodded. "It helps, but the race doesn't always go to the fastest horse, Ashleigh. It goes to the horse who runs the best race."

"Don't you have to get ready for school?" Mike's words tore her attention from the black colt on the track.

Ashleigh sighed. "Yes," she said, reluctant to leave. But if she missed the school bus, her parents would definitely forbid her ever to watch Aladdin's morning works again. Besides that, she had to get her project ready for the science fair.

•   •   •   •   •

"Way to go, Ashleigh." Lynne Duran set her lunch tray next to Mona's. "Your project was a hit. Where'd you come up with the wind resistance idea?"

Ashleigh dropped her eyes. "Oh," she said casually, "I did a little research."

Lynne unwrapped her hamburger and peeled back the top bun. She squinted at the patty, then sniffed it. "Wow. It looks like real meat for once." She reassembled the burger. "So, are you two going to the schooling show at Bluefield on Wednesday?"

Mona nodded while she chewed a bite of turkey sandwich. "There's no pairs class, but we're going to do the hunter course and the equitation flat class, right, Ash?"

Ashleigh paused in midbite. She narrowed her eyes and stared at Mona. "What do you mean, no pairs? You said we were jumping in a pairs class again."

Mona nodded. "I know, but I found a copy of the schedule last night. There aren't any pairs classes. But that's okay, isn't it? You still want to go, right?"

Ashleigh took a long swallow of milk. No pairs class. But after talking her parents into letting her go to another show, and asking for jumps and lessons, she couldn't quit now. Besides, she had to show that girl, Debbie, that her first blue ribbon was more than just beginner's luck.

Mona looked at her expectantly.

"Of course we're going," Ashleigh said with forced enthusiasm. "I can hardly wait." She looked at Lynne. "Are you and Jamie going, too?" Lynne and Jamie kept their horses at a boarding stable near town.

Lynne stuck out her lower lip. "I don't think so. Lance threw a shoe. I have to wait until the farrier comes before I can ride him. And Jamie's cold is still pretty bad. Maybe by next weekend we'll be able to go to a show."

Finally the school day ended. Ashleigh stared out the bus window, watching white-fenced pastures slip from view. In many of them mares and foals grazed and rested. When the bus passed a training farm, Ashleigh watched a rider galloping a bay Thoroughbred around a track. *Someday,* she thought, *that will be me.* But to Ashleigh that day seemed a very long way off.

When she got off the bus, Ashleigh ran up the tree-lined drive. She had to hurry and get Stardust tacked up so she could practice jumping before dark. If she was going to be showing in real hunter classes, she needed to practice. Caroline was on the kitchen phone when Ashleigh walked into the house. When she came back downstairs after changing her clothes, Caroline had not moved.

"That phone is going to get stuck to your head," Ashleigh teased just before she stepped outside. Caroline stuck her tongue out at her sister.

Mrs. Griffen was talking to Jonas outside the paddocks, and Mike was cleaning out his horse van. Ashleigh hurried past them shouting hellos. On her way to Stardust's stall she paused to visit Aladdin. The big black stallion seemed comfortable in his temporary home. His head was down, his eyes half closed, as he relaxed in the cool quiet of the barn. If he wanted to, he could look over his stall door and see out to where the mares and foals were turned out. Moe stood in the stall across the aisle, munching on a flake of hay.

"You don't mind being stuck in here with Aladdin, do you, Moe?" She rubbed the pony's fuzzy brown ears. Moe blew a loud snort in her direction and buried his nose in the hay.

"As long as you have lots of hay, you'd stay in here for weeks, wouldn't you?"

Stardust whinnied a greeting from down the aisle.

"Hey there, girl. Here I come," Ashleigh called, and hurried to get her mare ready.

By the time she reached the Gardeners', Mona was trotting Frisky over the cavaletti poles, and Ashleigh stopped to watch them for a minute. Mona looked very polished—head up, eyes forward, and hands low on Frisky's neck.

Ashleigh walked Stardust across the paddock, urging her into a trot when she reached the rail. She moved into the proper jumping position and aimed Stardust toward the center of the cavaletti poles. Stardust arched her neck, picking each hoof up with care, and trotted neatly over the poles.

"You know, Ash, you're starting to look really professional," Mona said, stopping Frisky to watch.

"Thanks," Ashleigh said, sitting upright and bringing the mare to a stop. "I want to do well on Wednesday."

Mona nodded. "Me too." But then she frowned. "What if it comes to a jump-off between you and me? Would we still be best friends?"

Ashleigh laughed. "You know we would. I'd be happy if you won. But I'd be happy if I won, too."

Mona looked relieved. "That's how I feel," she said. She pointed at the new course of homemade jumps laid out in the paddock. "See what my dad did for us?"

Mr. Gardener had rearranged the jumps so that they were spaced differently and the jumps themselves were more interesting, too. Two jumps were set at a diagonal across the middle of the ring, with only a few strides between them. The jump at the far end of the ring had a hay bale beneath it, making it look even more imposing. The last jump in the course was higher than it had been before, and some pine boughs had been scattered on the ground beneath it.

Ashleigh circled the paddock with Stardust, checking out the new setup. She watched as Mona began to canter Frisky around the new course, easily sailing over the hay-bale jump.

Then Mona guided Frisky through the turn and across the diagonal over the two jumps, taking three even strides between them. The last jump was to the right at the other end of the ring. Frisky landed and swapped leads, making her way to the last jump on her right lead. Like Stardust, Frisky was more flexible on her left side, and Ashleigh could see that changing leads made the jumps more of a challenge, but Frisky managed the last brush jump with a foot to spare.

"Way to go, Mona!" Ashleigh clapped.

"It's a good thing we do all those figure eights up on the flat," Mona said breathlessly, pulling Frisky up next to Stardust. "All that practice on our lead changes really makes a difference."

"Our turn," Ashleigh said determinedly.

She picked up her reins and nudged Stardust out to the rail at a walk before pressing her gently into a canter. Ashleigh felt her hands tighten on the reins when they approached the hay-bale jump. *We can do this,* she told herself, trying to relax. But Stardust hesitated before popping over the jump. They cleared it, though Stardust landed roughly, bouncing Ashleigh onto her withers.

Ashleigh quickly pushed herself back up and tried to gather her reins and straighten Stardust out before they made their turn across the diagonal. Stardust's ears were pricked with excitement, but she dropped back a notch, listening to Ashleigh's commands.

Ashleigh focused her eyes just above the second jump, and they flew over it. The third jump came up too quickly, and instead of putting in three strides, Stardust managed only two and a half. Again Ashleigh was thrown forward, and this time she lost a stirrup. She let the stirrup dangle and concentrated on getting Stardust on the right lead to the last jump.

Stardust cross-cantered through the turn and, after a few awkward hops, made the change with only a few strides to spare before the brush jump. Mr. Gardener had raised the jump only about six inches, but it seemed a lot scarier than the two-foot jumps. *What if Stardust catches a hoof and goes down?* Ashleigh fretted, but quickly she pushed the negative thought out of her mind.

Mona and Frisky cleared the jump with plenty of room, she told herself, and aimed for the center of the jump. She grabbed Stardust's mane and hung on for dear life as the mare left out a stride, sailing through the air and catching the rail with her back hoof. The rail came down with a thud and rolled along the ground behind them as they cantered away, like a reminder of their poor performance.

Ashleigh pulled Stardust to a walk and patted her neck. "We'll get it, girl," she said shakily, wishing she felt more confident. "I know we can do this." She looked at Mona and caught her lower lip in her teeth. "Do we have to change directions at the show?" she asked.

"We might," Mona said. "Especially if it comes to a jump-off. Don't worry, Ash. You just need to remember the steps to a good jump: approach, takeoff, suspension, landing, and recovery."

"Recovery," Ashleigh repeated, and laughed. "That's where I grab Stardust's mane to keep from slipping off."

Mona laughed, too. "You're doing great. Just wait until you start taking lessons with the rest of us. It'll get easier. You'll see."

They spent the rest of the afternoon working on alternating leads between jumps. When it was time for Ashleigh to go home, she and Stardust almost had the hang of it.

"Approach, takeoff, suspension, landing, recovery," Ashleigh recited to herself as she rode back to Edgardale. By the time they reached the barn, she had mentally jumped Stardust over every twig, leaf, and pebble in their path.

"Oh, Stardust," she said, sliding off the mare's back. "We have only one more day to practice. I hope I don't let you down. We can do this, can't we?"

6

The next afternoon Ashleigh stepped off the school bus and hurried toward the house, swinging her backpack. Overhead, the leafy trees filtered out the sun, keeping it cool and shady along the driveway.

She needed to get Stardust over to Mona's so that they could work on their jumping again before the show. One more day of practice wasn't nearly enough, but it was all she had. The thought of jumping all by herself, without Mona and Frisky at her side, still made Ashleigh nervous, but Mona made it seem so easy—Ashleigh just had to keep her confidence up.

As she neared the house she noticed Mike had Aladdin outside the barn, and the colt was saddled. Jumping forgotten, Ashleigh broke into a run toward the house. Maybe Mike would let her get up on Aladdin! Even if she could just walk him around one of the paddocks, it would be great. Ashleigh hurried upstairs to change. Caroline was at her desk, reading a book.

"Where are Mom and Rory?" Ashleigh asked, pulling off her sneakers.

"Mom took him to the community center to sign up for swimming lessons. Remember when we did that?"

Ashleigh pulled her old jeans on, nodding vigorously. "I still remember how excited I was when I put my face underwater and opened my eyes the first time."

"Yeah, me too," Caroline said, flipping a page in her textbook.

"Don't you get tired of studying so much?" Ashleigh asked, tugging a T-shirt over her head.

Caroline scribbled some notes on a sheet of paper. "I like my classes," she said. "History and English are fun, so it isn't hard."

Ashleigh threw a sweatshirt on over her head and pulled it down. "I guess science is kind of fun, but I'd still rather muck out stalls any day," she said. "See you." She dashed out of the room and down the stairs two at a time, reaching the barn just in time to see Mike hand Aladdin's saddle to a redheaded girl in chaps. Sam was standing at the colt's head and rubbing his nose.

Ashleigh slowed to a walk. They were putting

Aladdin away. Her shoulders slumped. So much for talking Mike into letting her ride him around the paddock.

Mike looked across Aladdin's back at her. "Ashleigh, this is Meghan McMackin," he said. Ashleigh recognized her as the exercise rider who had worked Aladdin at the Shady Valley track the morning before. "Sam talked her into coming over to take Aladdin out for us this afternoon."

"Hi," Ashleigh said, looking the other girl over. Even though she was older, maybe fifteen or sixteen, Meghan wasn't any bigger than Ashleigh. Ashleigh wondered how she could be strong enough to keep such a powerful racehorse under control.

"Meghan took him up the lanes for a jog, just to get him out of his stall for a while," Sam said. "Mike and I thought it might do the guy's spirit some good."

"Aladdin's awesome," Meghan said, stroking the colt's shoulder. "I'm so glad I get to ride him, even if it is just to exercise him."

"I can hardly wait until I'm old enough to be an exercise rider," Ashleigh said enviously. "Just think—you're only one step away from being a jockey."

Sam looked from Meghan to Ashleigh. "Meghan has been exercise-riding at Shady Valley for almost two years now, Ashleigh. Maybe in a couple more years you could start working there, too."

Ashleigh smiled, but the smile felt forced. Two more years—that was an eternity! She didn't know if she could stand waiting that long.

Meghan laughed. "A couple of years sounds like forever, doesn't it?" she asked, as if she'd read Ashleigh's mind. "That's exactly how I feel about getting my jockey's license. It seems like it's going to take a lifetime."

Ashleigh really liked Meghan. "Maybe if you take Aladdin out here again, I could go with you," she suggested. "I could ride my horse, Stardust."

Meghan turned to Mike. "Do you want me to come back tomorrow afternoon?"

Mike nodded. "It helps his mental state to get him out like that. We'll be bringing him over to Shady Valley in the morning, and then in the afternoon you could come over and take him along the lanes again." He glanced at Ashleigh. "But you're riding in another show tomorrow afternoon, aren't you?"

Ashleigh grimaced. She had forgotten the Bluefield show. She'd promised Mona she'd go, so she couldn't back out now. It would be fantastic to ride with Meghan and Aladdin, but she had to let the idea go.

"You're right. I forgot. I do have a show," she admitted. "But I'm definitely going to Shady Valley in the morning to watch Aladdin work. Anyway, I'd better get over to Mona's now. She's waiting for me."

"Maybe we can ride together some other time," Meghan said.

"That would be great," Ashleigh said. "See you later."

She headed into the barn for Stardust's halter. Stardust and Moe were grooming each other in their turnout. Ashleigh laughed at the sight of the little pony stretching his neck to nuzzle the mare's shoulder. "Come on, Stardust," she said, slipping into the paddock. "We need to get over to Mona's."

She led Stardust into the barn. As they approached Aladdin's stall, Ashleigh noticed his bright blue blanket hanging from a hook on the wall. A current of air wafted through the barn, stirring the blanket.

Just as they reached the crossties in front of the stall, a strong gust of wind whipped through the open aisle. Aladdin's blanket snapped in the breeze and billowed like a sail. Stardust gave a loud snort and jumped sideways, nearly pulling free from Ashleigh's hold.

Ashleigh gripped the lead, bringing the mare to a halt. Stardust snorted, trembling, as she stared at the blanket, her eyes wide.

"Steady, girl," Ashleigh said, keeping the startled horse facing the rustling sheet. She reached up to stroke the mare's shoulder. "It's just a horse blanket."

"What's going on?" Mike and Aladdin appeared in

the doorway of the barn. He frowned at Stardust. Her neck was arched as she kept a wary eye on the blanket.

"She just spooked a little," Ashleigh said.

"Is she always so jumpy?" Mike asked, returning Aladdin to his stall.

"No," Ashleigh said, her face heating up. Why did Stardust have to act like such a baby sometimes? "She's much better than she used to be."

Mike busied himself mixing a feed pan of grain and supplements for Aladdin, and Ashleigh put Stardust in the crossties and started to groom her. The mare began to relax when Ashleigh stroked her with the soft brush.

"You can't spend your life spooking at every little thing you see, Stardust. We need to do something about this." She rubbed Stardust's white-starred forehead, and the mare bobbed her head.

She led Stardust out to the paddock they had used the past winter as a makeshift round pen. Stardust nuzzled her head into Ashleigh's chest.

"Don't try to make up to me now," Ashleigh said firmly. "You can't jump out of your skin every time something catches you by surprise. It's dangerous."

She eyed the mare for a minute, thinking. Then it dawned on her, and Ashleigh hurried back into the barn. She dug through a pile of empty feed bags until she found a tattered blue tarp. "This should work," she muttered, returning to Stardust.

Ashleigh showed Stardust the folded tarp. Stardust smelled it, lipped it, and let Ashleigh rub it along her neck. Stardust trembled, her eyes rolling warily, but she stood still. Then Ashleigh unfolded the tarp and flapped it in the air. When Stardust jumped away with a startled snort, Ashleigh dropped the tarp and sent the mare off, waving her arms until Stardust was cantering around the pen. After a few trips around, Stardust wheeled in and stopped in front of Ashleigh, snorting and shaking her head.

When Ashleigh first got Stardust, the mare had spooked at everything she saw and heard, and Ashleigh had spent more time on the ground than in the saddle. It had been very frustrating. But after reading a few books and watching a few videos, Ashleigh had tried working Stardust in a round pen, and slowly they learned to trust each other. Whenever Stardust began acting up again, Ashleigh went back to the round pen. It was hard work, but it was worth it.

"I should have been doing this while I was grounded last month," Ashleigh said. "I guess you need to go over your lessons once in a while, too, just like me with math."

Ashleigh rubbed the mare's nose, then waved the tarp again. When Stardust spooked once more, Ashleigh sent her cantering around the paddock again.

After a few times of having the tarp flapped in her face, Stardust finally just snorted and sniffed it rather than jumping away.

"Atta girl," Ashleigh crowed. She draped the tarp over Stardust's back and dragged it over her head. Stardust kept an eye on the strange piece of material, but she didn't spook again.

"That's great!"

At Mike's voice, Ashleigh spun around, her cheeks pink. "How long have you been watching us?" she demanded.

"For a while," Mike said. "You're a good horse trainer, Ashleigh."

Ashleigh felt pride well up inside her. Coming from Mike, that was the greatest compliment in the world. "Thanks." She walked over to the fence and Stardust followed, though Ashleigh wasn't carrying a lead.

"I figured if she thought she had to work every time she spooked, she'd eventually stop spooking," Ashleigh said, refolding the tarp.

Mike nodded. "I think you have the right idea," he said. "Maybe sometime you can show me some of the other things you're doing with her. I'm always open to learning new things."

Ashleigh gave Mike a quick look. "Sure," she said, surprised that Mike thought he could learn something from her.

"Here, let me give you a hand tacking her up so you can go ride," Mike said, opening the gate.

With Mike's help, Stardust was ready to go in minutes, and Ashleigh headed for Mona's to practice jumping. She was still riding high from Mike's compliments, so this time the course didn't look so intimidating. They went back and forth over the big brushy jump until it felt like no big deal, and Ashleigh rode home confident that she would do well in the Bluefield show the following day.

It was difficult to get up so early in the morning, but the thought of seeing Aladdin work drove Ashleigh from her bed. She dressed quickly and slipped outside. She didn't bother going to the barn, but hopped on her bicycle and pedaled as fast as she could to Shady Valley. Meghan was already on Aladdin, jogging him around the track. Mike and Sam were watching intently, side by side at the rail.

"Morning, Ashleigh," Sam said, leaning an elbow on the top rail of the fence. He watched Meghan move Aladdin into a canter and nodded. "She's a natural."

Mike nodded. "Definitely has a knack for working with the horses," he said. "And it helps that she's got a great coach, too."

Ashleigh watched Meghan restrain Aladdin as the horse circled the track at an easy gallop. The big colt arched his neck and huffed, trying to tug the reins free from Meghan's grip.

"How can she be strong enough to hold him?" Ashleigh asked. "I mean, she's my size, and I couldn't control him."

"It takes time and practice, Ashleigh," Sam said. "Don't worry, you'll get there. Meghan does some weight lifting, and she does gymnastics to help her balance and coordination."

Ashleigh watched the horse and rider gallop around the track again, mentally positioning her own body as if she were balancing on a racing saddle. She wished she could spend all day talking racing and horses with Mike, Sam, and Meghan. But she was only ten—she had to go to school. And after school was the Bluefield show. Somehow the show didn't seem all that thrilling compared to what Meghan was doing right then. *But I can't let Mona and Stardust down,* Ashleigh thought. *I've got to do my best.*

After school Ashleigh raced to the barn and flung her backpack down in the aisle. She had less than an hour to get Stardust groomed and her mane braided before Mrs. Gardener and Mona came to pick her up for the show.

She stopped at the barn door. Her mother had Stardust in crossties and was trimming the mare's fetlocks with electric clippers. Stardust had been given a complete makeover and was looking fabulous. Her mane was braided, her coat was clipped and groomed, and her whole body glowed with a coppery sheen.

"Wow," Ashleigh said, walking slowly up to her horse.

Mrs. Griffen glanced at Ashleigh. "So you think I did a good job?"

"She looks amazing!" Ashleigh exclaimed.

"I don't think she'd recognize herself if she looked in the mirror. Would you, Stardust?" her mother said with a laugh. "Now, you'd better get your clothes together and get ready to go." She rose and shooed Ashleigh toward the door. "I'll wrap her legs."

"You're the best!" Ashleigh called, and hurried out of the barn to get dressed.

When Ashleigh led Stardust from the trailer at Bluefield, the mare lifted her head and smelled the air. "No different from last Sunday, girl," Ashleigh said, and patted her shoulder.

The show ground consisted of two large oval rings side by side in a field, with a short set of bleachers at either side. One of the rings was filled with jumps, and the other was reserved for under-saddle classes. Behind the bleachers on the far side, a few practice jumps were set up in the field. The adult classes had been in session all day, and the show was in full swing. Now that school was over, trailers and vans were pulling in from all directions and unloading children and their ponies and horses. There weren't many hours to go before dark, and the announcer was eager to get the children's classes under way. "Novice riders, please have your mounts at the gate as soon as possible," he called.

"Come on. Let's get the horses saddled and warmed up," Mona said, holding Frisky's lead.

Ashleigh was relieved to see the jumps were pretty straightforward compared to the course at Mona's. She knew she wasn't ready for anything harder, especially since she and Stardust would be all alone out there.

They trotted their horses in a circle around the practice jumps, and then took turns popping back and forth over a low cross rail. Stardust was alert and listening. Ashleigh brought her back to a walk and patted her neck. "Good girl," she said nervously as Mona led the way to the jumping ring.

Mona had signed them up for the first class. She was second to ride, and Ashleigh was fifth on the program. She sat on Stardust, watching as Mona trotted into the ring and began to jump the course. Mona positioned Frisky perfectly for the first jump, and they sailed over it. Ashleigh could see her friend's eyes already looking toward the second jump while she was still in the air.

"She's really good."

Ashleigh turned around at the familiar voice. It was Danielle, standing by the rail on her black Thoroughbred. Beyond them Ashleigh could see Danielle's nasty friend, Debbie, holding her horse. The show vet was bent by the mare's leg, examining her.

"Mona works really hard," Ashleigh agreed. "And Frisky is an amazing horse."

When Mona was finished with her round, Ashleigh and Danielle dropped their reins and clapped for her. Ashleigh could see Mrs. Gardener beaming and applauding for her daughter from the bleachers. Beside her were Ashleigh's own parents, who had arrived and were clapping, too, with Rory and Caroline beside them. Rory waved to her, and Ashleigh waved back. Caroline looked bored, but Ashleigh was glad she had come anyway.

Mona walked out of the ring, grinning from ear to ear and patting Frisky gratefully on the neck.

"Keep this area clear for the next rider!" the gate steward called out.

Mona pointed, motioning to Ashleigh that she'd be waiting on the other side of the ring until the class was over. Ashleigh nodded that she understood.

"Mona loves to jump more than anything," Ashleigh said to Danielle as the next rider started her course.

"Me too," Danielle agreed.

Ashleigh looked admiringly at Danielle's horse and again wondered about his bloodlines. "Your horse looks like a Thoroughbred. Was he ever a racehorse?" she asked.

Danielle nodded. "Yes, but he didn't do much on the track."

Before Ashleigh could ask another question, it was Danielle's turn. She picked up her reins and guided her horse into the ring. They moved into a slow, rocking canter, gliding easily over each jump as though it were the easiest thing in the world. Ashleigh watched nervously. It was her turn next.

Ashleigh tried to focus on staying relaxed, but Stardust tossed her head as they circled the ring, and she felt her knees tighten. She breathed out, trying not to communicate her tension down the reins, but she could feel her hands trembling as they headed for the first jump.

"We can do this," she murmured to Stardust, shifting into jumping position. Stardust took off too soon, but they cleared the jump and cantered away. Ashleigh gritted her teeth and headed the mare for the next obstacle. Stardust sailed over it like a pro.

Ashleigh was just sitting back onto the saddle when a little boy ran past the ring, a shiny helium balloon bobbing in the air above him. Ashleigh could feel Stardust tense as the mare caught the movement of the balloon from the corner of her eye. Ashleigh quickly turned the mare toward the next jump before she could react to the distraction.

After the third jump Stardust seemed to settle down, and they finished the course without any major faults. Ashleigh rode out through the gate, relieved just to have gotten around the ring without making a fool of herself. She was too nervous to have really enjoyed it.

"That was good, Ash," Mona said as Ashleigh rode up beside her.

"Yeah, but I thought I was going to get dumped when Stardust saw that balloon," Ashleigh said. "I hope someone makes the kid put it away."

A smattering of applause made Ashleigh look up at the ring. The last rider had just finished the course.

One by one the announcer called the riders back for their ribbons. Mona's name was called for the blue ribbon—she had come in first! Danielle and her black gelding came in second, and Ashleigh was fifth. When the steward pinned the pink ribbon on Stardust's bridle, Ashleigh looked up at the bleachers, grinning, and saw her family clapping for her. She had done all right after all.

Next was the hunt-seat equitation class. Flat work was a lot easier for Ashleigh than jumping, and she breezed through the judge's instructions. Some of the riders struggled with their sitting trot, but Stardust's smooth gait made it easy.

When the judge began to eliminate riders one by one, she, Danielle, and Mona, along with a boy and two other girls, were the only ones left in the ring. They lined their horses up side by side in the center of the ring and waited for the announcer to call out the results. First one of the other girls was handed the sixth-place ribbon. Then the boy and another girl received the fifth- and fourth-place ribbons. From the corner of her eye, Ashleigh saw a flicker of disappointment on Danielle's face when the judge pinned the third-place ribbon on her horse's headstall.

That means Mona gets the blue and I get the red, Ashleigh thought.

But the judge clipped the red ribbon to Frisky's headstall. Ashleigh felt a wave of giddy excitement run through her. It seemed unreal when the judge smiled at her and fixed the blue ribbon on Stardust's bridle.

"Wow," she murmured disbelievingly.

The assistant winked at her, and Ashleigh grinned back.

When they rode out of the ring, her parents were at the gate.

"Congratulations, sweetheart," her mother said, smiling up at her. "You looked great."

"Thanks, Mom." Ashleigh swung off Stardust's back.

Her father smiled proudly. "We thought we'd pick up a celebratory pizza on our way home," he said. "Pepperoni and mushroom, right?"

Ashleigh nodded. "My favorite," she said with a grin.

"We'll see you at home, then," her mother said, giving Stardust a pat. Ashleigh watched them walk away, smiling to herself. Showing was turning out to be pretty fun after all.

"We'll see how well you do at the show this weekend."

Ashleigh looked up to see Debbie watching her. Ashleigh realized Debbie hadn't ridden in any of the classes, though she was dressed in immaculate show clothes, as usual.

"Is your horse okay?" Ashleigh asked. Debbie wasn't very nice, but Ashleigh did care about her horse.

Debbie looked surprised. "She'll be okay," she said. "The vet said it's just a stone bruise. We'll be riding again this weekend." She turned and walked away quickly.

Ashleigh watched her go, then turned to Mona, who was leading Frisky toward her. "Where's the show this weekend?"

"There are two days of classes this weekend. But it's an A-rated show, Ash. Do you think you're ready? It would be great if you want to try it."

"I really want to go," Ashleigh said. "It can't be that much harder than this, can it?"

"I'll get my mom to sign us up," Mona said eagerly, leading Frisky toward the trailer. "I'm so glad you're getting into jumping, Ash. We'll be able to go to shows every weekend, and we can take lessons together after school."

Ashleigh slowed. Every weekend? She'd never get to see another horse race if she went to all the shows with Mona.

Mona flashed her a bright smile. "This is going to be so cool, Ashleigh." She held up the ribbons she'd won that day. "Frisky and Stardust are going to have the best-decorated stalls in the state!"

Ashleigh gazed at the fluttering ribbons, then glanced at the pink and blue ones she'd won. Mona was right, she decided. Showing was a lot of fun, and she and Stardust were getting better and better. Her dreams of being a jockey were such a long way off. The track would just have to wait.

When Ashleigh walked into the hous119
e on Thursday afternoon, Mrs. Danworth was sitting
at the kitchen table with Ashleigh's mother, looking
over breeding charts.

"Hello, Ashleigh." Mrs. Danworth smiled warmly at
her, but Ashleigh suddenly felt shy. With her fashion-
able clothes and elegantly styled hair, Peter's mother
looked out of place in the Griffens' kitchen.

"Hi," Ashleigh said. She struggled to think of something else to say. "Have you seen Aladdin yet?" was the
best she could come up with.

Mrs. Danworth smiled. "Yes, and he looks quite
content. You've taken excellent care of him. Peter's
with him right now."

Ashleigh started toward the stairs. Maybe Peter
was going to take Aladdin out on the lanes that afternoon, and she and Stardust could go along. But at the

sharp look her mother gave her, she stopped.

"May I go down to the barn now?" she asked, trying to remember her manners.

"Don't let us keep you from your horses," Mrs. Danworth said, giving Ashleigh a wink. "The weather is too nice to be stuck inside with us, going over pedigrees."

"I have something for you first," her mother said.

The shopping bag her mother held up was from the local tack store. Ashleigh took the package and opened it eagerly. "A shirt?" she said, giving her mother a quizzical look when she saw the neatly pressed high-collared blouse.

"A ratcatcher," her mother said. "For all your horse shows."

"Wow! Thanks, Mom!" Ashleigh gave her mother a quick hug and hurried upstairs. Caroline was nowhere to be seen, but their bathroom door was closed, and Ashleigh could hear the shower going. Ashleigh pulled on her boots, then hung her new shirt neatly in her closet before she dashed out of the house and headed for the barn.

Aladdin stood in the crossties while Peter brushed his shiny black coat. Rory was running a soft cloth down the colt's front legs. Aladdin had his head lowered and his eyes half closed. Ashleigh smiled at how content the horse looked.

"Hey, Peter," she said, careful not to startle Aladdin.

"Look, Ashleigh," Rory said. "Peter's letting me help him."

"I see that," Ashleigh said. "It looks like you're doing a great job, Rory."

"He is," Peter said, rubbing the stallion's gleaming neck. "Aladdin doesn't look like the same horse we brought here last Saturday, does he?"

"Not at all," Ashleigh said. "He's really calm now." She tugged on the stallion's mane. "Just don't start thinking you're an old plow horse, Aladdin. You still have to get out there and win on Sunday." She rubbed his poll with her fingers, gently massaging around the base of his ears. The horse leaned toward her.

"Oh, he will," Peter said confidently. "You're looking at the next winner of the Keeneland Mile. I just hope Dad and Mike can straighten out the stall arrangements there soon. Aladdin needs time to get used to the place, and Mike wants me to ride him there a couple times before the race."

Ashleigh knew Aladdin needed to get settled at the track, but secretly she wished he could stay at Edgardale longer.

She watched Peter run the brush along Aladdin's neck. He didn't even have to reach up to groom the horse's withers. Poor Peter. He'd always wanted to be a jockey, but he was already too tall.

"Are you going to take him out this afternoon?" she asked. "I'll get his saddle for you."

Before Peter could reply, Caroline came into the barn.

Ashleigh gaped at her sister. Caroline had her hair twisted and clipped into a style a cover model from a teen magazine would wear. She was wearing a fuzzy pink sweater with her jeans and paddock shoes. Ashleigh wanted to point out how totally impractical her sweater was for cleaning stalls, but then she glanced at Peter. He didn't seem to mind the way Caroline looked.

"Hi, Peter," Caroline said, flashing him a brilliant smile. "How's Aladdin doing?"

Ashleigh scowled at both of them. Peter wasn't going to talk about horses with her when Caroline was around.

"He's great," Peter said. "Rory and I were just going to walk him up the paddock lanes. Do you want to come?"

"I'd love to," Caroline said, furrowing her brow. "But I have stalls to clean."

Ashleigh wanted to point out that her sister had taken a shower and gotten dressed up just to muck her stalls, but she held back. She didn't want to embarrass Caroline.

"I'll help you do your stalls after we walk Big Al," Peter offered.

Caroline gave Peter another blinding smile. "That would be great!"

"Ashleigh, want to come?" Peter asked.

"Sorry," Ashleigh explained. "I have to do my stalls, and then I'm meeting Mona."

Ashleigh watched Peter and her sister walk out of the barn with Aladdin. Rory clung to Peter's free hand, looking up at the older boy as though he were a superhero. She turned away, trying not to feel left out.

But as she cleaned her stalls, Ashleigh couldn't get the image of Caroline in her silly pink sweater out of her mind. She cleaned her assigned stalls, picked up Stardust's halter, and headed for the paddock. "Caroline could care less about Aladdin," Ashleigh told the mare. "I don't know why she has to start acting like that when Peter's around."

Stardust nudged Ashleigh, who absently rubbed her nose and murmured, "I know, girl. You don't care about that stuff, do you?"

"And it's star rider Ashleigh Griffen on Stardust, with a clean round in the jump-off!" Mona trumpeted. Stardust flew over the brush with nearly a foot to spare. Ashleigh felt as though they were flying.

"You look really good," Mona said when Ashleigh stopped Stardust beside Frisky.

"Thanks, Mona," Ashleigh said, rubbing Stardust's neck. "I think we're getting the hang of it."

"Listen, we still have time to go for a trail ride," Mona said. "We don't want the horses to get burned out jumping."

"Let's go!" Ashleigh readily agreed.

They rode side by side across the field. "So you still want to go to the show this weekend, right?" Mona asked. "Preregistration has to be in by tonight."

Ashleigh nodded. "Yes. And I'm sure I can do even better than yesterday."

"I'll ask my mom to get us signed up, then," Mona said.

They galloped the mares along a wide trail. Ashleigh leaned forward, urging Stardust to run fast. Frisky galloped alongside her, easily keeping up with her long Thoroughbred stride. It felt so good to run that Ashleigh didn't want to stop, but the horses were tired from jumping. After a short gallop the girls turned back, walking the horses back to the Gardeners' barn. "See you at school tomorrow," Ashleigh called, waving good-bye as she started down the driveway.

After settling Stardust in her stall, Ashleigh hurried through the barn. Aladdin's stall was empty, but she heard voices outside, so she headed for the back paddock. When she stepped outside, she stopped cold. Peter was leading Aladdin around the paddock, and Caroline was sitting on the big stallion's back.

Before they saw her, Ashleigh ducked back into the barn and ran down the aisle and up to the house, fuming. Peter was letting Caroline ride Aladdin! It was beyond unfair. She hurried upstairs and tried to do her homework, angrily staring at her textbooks until her mother called her down to dinner.

Mr. Danworth and Mr. Griffen had spent the afternoon at Keeneland with Mike, and they brought home Chinese food for dinner. With the Danworths at the table, the meal was a hectic mix of conversations. Ashleigh wanted to hear what the Danworths had to say about the race, but every time she looked at Caroline and Peter, they had their heads together and were laughing. Rory sat close to them, laughing whenever the teenagers did.

"What do you think of putting a claim on Bold's Dark Star in the first race on Sunday?" Ashleigh's father asked her mother. "The claiming price isn't very high for a horse with her bloodlines."

Ashleigh snapped to attention and turned away from Peter and Caroline. She recognized the horse's name. Was her dad serious about putting a claim on her?

"She's won only one race out of five starts," her

mother said. "Do you really think she'd enhance our breeding program?"

"But she's good on dirt," Ashleigh broke in. "And she's a distance horse. She wasn't meant for those five-and-a-half-furlong races."

Her parents and the Danworths all looked down the table at Ashleigh, their eyebrows raised in surprise.

She ducked her head and blushed. "I've been reading up on her in the *Daily Racing Form,*" she said.

"And don't forget, she and Aladdin share some bloodlines," Mr. Danworth added, smiling at Ashleigh. "They both have Bold Ruler as a grandsire. Anyway, we'll see how she goes on Sunday. Her race is just before Aladdin's."

Ashleigh fumbled with her chopsticks, excited about the prospect of a new mare on the farm. Then she stopped, dropping her chopsticks on her plate. *Sunday.* Aladdin's race was on Sunday, and she was supposed to be at a horse show! Ashleigh's mind raced. What should she do?

"I can't believe Caroline rode Aladdin," Lynne said from across the cafeteria table.

Mona sat beside Lynne, shaking her head as Ashleigh told them what had happened the day before. Around them, the steady hum of voices and the clatter of dishes filled the lunchroom.

"I can't believe it, either," Ashleigh said, carefully dissecting a peanut butter cookie. "Yesterday she was acting as though horses were her entire life, but she doesn't even like them. And Peter knows I'd do anything for another chance to get on Aladdin, but he didn't even ask me."

"But technically she didn't really ride him," Mona said quickly. "Peter just led them around the paddock, right?"

Ashleigh nodded. She knew Mona was trying to make her feel better, but she was still upset.

"You're both going to the show at Eaton Stables this weekend, aren't you?" Lynne asked. When Ashleigh and Mona nodded, she frowned. "Well, I'm not." She rose and picked up her tray. "The farrier had to reschedule. And since Jamie is still sick, there's no way her parents will let her go."

"That's too bad," Mona said. "The next rated show is a month from now."

"I know." Lynne shrugged. "But I think there are a couple of schooling shows before that. I can't wait to start showing again." She glanced at Ashleigh. "Isn't it great, Ash?"

Ashleigh stood up and nodded absentmindedly,

but her mind was on other things. She'd promised Mona she'd go to the show, but how could she when it was Aladdin's race day? She'd hardly spent any time with Aladdin since he'd been at Edgardale, and he'd be leaving soon. *As soon as I get home I'm going to ask Peter if I can take Aladdin around one of the paddocks, too.* If he let Caroline ride him, he couldn't say no to her.

"You're still coming over to practice this afternoon, aren't you?" Mona asked as the school bus slowed at the Griffens' driveway that afternoon.

"I'll be there as soon as I can," Ashleigh called, jumping up. She hurried off the bus and raced up to the house, nearly colliding with Caroline, who was coming out the kitchen door.

"Watch out!" Caroline exclaimed, stepping out of Ashleigh's way.

"Sorry," Ashleigh gasped as she rushed past her sister.

She changed quickly, but when she got outside she saw that the Danworths' horse van was gone. She dashed inside the barn, but before she got halfway down the aisle she could see Peter in Aladdin's stall, a pitchfork in his hands. Beside him was a wheelbarrow full of soiled bedding.

"Is Aladdin gone?"

"Yup." Peter threw a forkful of bedding into the wheelbarrow. "Dad and Mike took him to the track a couple hours ago. Mom and I are driving into Lexington after I'm done here. I'm working Big Al on the Keeneland track tomorrow morning."

"Great," Ashleigh said, swallowing a lump of disappointment.

"As soon as I'm done with Aladdin's stall, I told your brother I'd clean Moe's," Peter said, pushing the loaded cart into the aisle.

"That's okay," Ashleigh said. "I can take care of it."

"No problem," Peter replied. "I can do it."

"Hey, Peter, I found the other pitchfork!" Caroline called as she walked out of the tack room. "I'll give you a hand."

"Thanks," Peter answered. He dumped more wet bedding into the wheelbarrow. "Horses sure leave a big mess behind, don't they?"

Caroline laughed. "Boy, don't I know it! It seems like I spend half my life cleaning stalls."

Ashleigh turned away, disgusted. Caroline should have said she spent half her life trying to *avoid* cleaning stalls. She met Jonas coming down the aisle. The stable hand raised his eyebrows at her. "What's wrong, Ashleigh?" he asked.

"Nothing," she said. "I just wish Aladdin could have

stayed longer. I hardly got to spend any time with him."

Jonas nodded in understanding. "Well, you've been pretty busy with Stardust and going to shows," he said, looking down at her.

Peter walked by, pushing the wheelbarrow. Caroline was right beside him.

"Hi, Mr. McIntyre," Peter said as they passed.

"He's a nice young fellow," Jonas said to Ashleigh.

Ashleigh nodded, not trusting herself to speak.

"What kind of work are you going to do with Aladdin tomorrow?" she heard Caroline ask Peter.

"First thing," he said, "I need to warm him up by . . ." Peter's voice faded as they walked out of the barn.

Jonas rested a hand on her shoulder. "Mike is glad to have Aladdin at the track now. They've finally got him a good stall," he said. "It's not good to move a horse around just before a race. It's important to do what's best for the colt."

Ashleigh felt her shoulders slump. "I know," she said. "It's just that I'm going to miss him."

"Are you sure you're okay?" Jonas frowned at her. "Is something else bothering you?"

"I'm fine," Ashleigh said, even though it was hardly true. She didn't know how to put into words all that was troubling her. Aladdin was gone. She couldn't ride him in the paddock, and she might not see him again at all because of the Eaton show. Not only that, Caroline was completely monopolizing Peter . . . the list was endless.

"I need to get Stardust out," she said. Even if she didn't have a chance to ride Aladdin, she still had Stardust, and they had a show the next day. She picked up her pace, grabbing Stardust's halter as she passed the tack room.

When she opened the gate into Stardust's paddock, the mare came over, eagerly snuffing her hands. "Sorry, girl," she said. "I didn't bring you any treats today." She slipped the mare's halter on. "I'll bring you an apple later. Right now we have a lot of work to do."

She groomed Stardust and settled the saddle on her back, trying to concentrate on the show the next day and forget about Aladdin's being back at Keeneland. She trotted Stardust along the road and met Mona in front of the Gardeners' barn.

"We're signed up for both days of the show," Mona told her as they rode the horses into the paddock full of jumps. "Pairs jumping and novice hunters over fences and on the flat on Saturday, then hunt-seat equitation on the flat and over fences on Sunday." Mona grinned broadly. "I'm so glad we're doing this together. It's going to be a blast."

"Me too," Ashleigh agreed. "I guess we'd better practice, right?" Ashleigh started warming Stardust up at a trot, bending her neck and working her in figure eights. Then she followed Mona, circling over the cavaletti poles. Mona asked Frisky to canter, and Ashleigh pulled Stardust up to watch them jump the course. Mona's hands were light as Frisky cantered easily through the diagonal and around the final turn to the brush jump. Ashleigh walked Stardust out to the end of the ring and picked up the canter. She decide to jump the course backward, with the highest jump first. Stardust cleared all the jumps easily, and Ashleigh felt almost relaxed for the first time.

"Good one, Ash!" Mona called.

"We're going to win tomorrow, right, Stardust?" Ashleigh said, patting her mare. "No problem." She stopped Stardust next to Frisky.

Mona narrowed her eyes. "Don't be so sure, Ash," she said in a warning tone. "It isn't a schooling show, remember. It's going to be pretty tough competition."

"Don't worry," Ashleigh reassured her friend. "We can do it."

"Okay," Mona replied. "Then let's go up to the big pasture and work on our equitation. I *am* worried about that!"

"All right, but let's have a good run first. You know, just to get the kinks out," Ashleigh suggested.

"You got it," Mona agreed.

They walked their horses behind the Gardeners' barn and up a hill to a grassy meadow.

"One, two, three, go!" Ashleigh cried, nudging Stardust into a canter and then a gallop. Frisky caught up with her, and the two horses galloped over the grass side by side. The wind made tears stream from Ashleigh's eyes, and it whistled in her ears. It felt glorious!

By the time she rode home, Ashleigh was in a great mood. Riding with her best friend was so much fun, and she and Stardust had never been more ready to win.

When she sat down to dinner, the table seemed quiet without the Danworths there.

"What time are we leaving for the track tomorrow?" Caroline asked, handing Ashleigh a bowl heaped with steamed broccoli.

The bowl nearly slipped from Ashleigh's hands. "Tomorrow?" she exclaimed. "But the race isn't until Sunday."

Her father nodded. "We planned to go up and watch Aladdin work in the morning. And your mother and I have some other business to discuss with the Danworths as well."

"But I'm signed up for a show tomorrow," Ashleigh said.

"Well, then you'll just have to wait until Sunday's race," her father said, shrugging.

"It should be a really exciting race," Mrs. Griffen said, spooning out mashed potatoes for Rory.

Mr. Griffen nodded. "There are some fine three-year-olds running," he said. "The Keeneland Mile should be a good challenge for Aladdin."

Ashleigh listened in silence, chewing slowly. She couldn't deny it. She wanted to be there on Sunday to cheer Aladdin on at the Keeneland Mile.

"We're going to brunch with the Danworths Sunday morning, then in the afternoon we'll watch Aladdin race," Mrs. Griffen said. "Doesn't that sound like fun?"

Ashleigh's stomach sank. "It's a two-day A-rated show. I'm supposed to ride in the show on Sunday, too," she admitted, staring down at her plate.

"You're showing two days in a row?" Her father sounded surprised.

Ashleigh looked up at him and nodded. "Mona's mother already signed us up. But our classes are in the morning. I didn't think we were going to leave for the track until later."

Her father lowered his brows, giving her a serious look. "You're getting pretty caught up in this horse show business, aren't you?"

Ashleigh looked back at him. "I've only been to a

couple of schooling shows, Dad. And the show this weekend is A-rated."

"It will give Ashleigh a chance to see if she really enjoys showing, Derek," her mother said.

Mr. Griffen glanced from Mrs. Griffen to Ashleigh. "You're willing to miss seeing Aladdin run on Sunday?" he said, looking bewildered.

Ashleigh chewed on her lower lip. "I want to see him," she said quietly. "But I promised Mona I'd go to the show with her."

Mr. Griffen nodded. "Then you're going to have to make a decision, Ash. You can't be in both places at the same time."

Ashleigh slumped on her chair and poked at her food with her fork. She couldn't just back out of the show without hurting Mona's feelings. Besides, she wanted to go. But she'd miss Aladdin's race.

"I'm not hungry," she said finally, and set her fork down. "Can I go down to the barn and check on Stardust?"

Her mother nodded. "Go ahead," she said. "Just put your plate in the refrigerator. You can reheat it later if you want to."

Ashleigh walked down to the barn, which smelled sweet from the hay and the horses. She greeted the mares and foals, pausing at Go Gen's stall to admire Shadow. The little black filly was sleeping curled up at her mother's feet. Ashleigh watched quietly, not wanting to disturb her.

She continued on to Stardust's stall, stopping to finger her ribbons from the schooling shows. *My first blue ribbon with Stardust*, she thought, recalling her and Mona's dream of covering their horses' stalls with ribbons. *It won't happen if we don't ride at shows*, she reminded herself.

She slipped inside the stall and sat down in the thick bedding. Stardust pulled a bite from her flake of hay and swung her head in Ashleigh's direction. Ashleigh rested her cheek on her knee and watched the horse's jaw move rhythmically.

"If I go watch Aladdin race, I won't be able to ride you at the show on Sunday," she told her horse, who flicked her ears in Ashleigh's direction. "But I think we can win. Even if the classes are a little harder, I know you can do it." Stardust stopped chewing and blinked at Ashleigh. Then she sighed and went back to her hay. Ashleigh leaned back against the wall and looked up at the thick wooden beams in the barn's ceiling. "But I want to see Aladdin run, too," Ashleigh cried. "Oh, Stardust, I just don't know what to do."

8

"I think it's great you decided to try an A-rated show, Ashleigh," Mrs. Gardener said when Ashleigh climbed into the cab of the pickup on Saturday morning.

"Me too," Mona said, scooting over to give Ashleigh more room. "We're going to have a great time!" she said, grinning at Ashleigh. "Ribbons in every class, right?"

Ashleigh buckled her seat belt and shut the truck door. "I hope so," she said. She tugged at the collar of the ratcatcher her mother had given her. She still had the same old jodhpurs, boots, and jacket, but at least her shirt was nice and new. She sat back as they started down the driveway. The sun was shining, and a few puffy clouds floated in the sky. Mona was right. This was going to be a great day.

But when they arrived at the show grounds, her stomach sank. In a vast, beautifully manicured polo field three separate jumping rings had been set up, each one more elaborate than the next—one for hunters, one for jumpers, and one for the ponies. Ashleigh climbed from the truck, gazing at all the immaculately turned-out horses and riders in attendance. More than ever, Ashleigh felt as though she didn't belong.

"Let's check out the jumps," Mona said, leading the way to the hunter ring.

Ashleigh stared at the course. A blue-painted pool of fake water had been set up beneath one jump, creating what Mona called a liverpool. Ashleigh eyed the jump closely. She hoped the work she had done with Stardust would keep the mare from spooking at the strange obstacle. She looked around at the rest of the course. There were brush jumps and hay bales and flowers and stone walls. No plain rails at all. This was nothing like the schooling shows—this was more like the Olympics!

Mona leaned against the arena fence. "Aren't they neat?" She pointed at a jump that looked like two wishing wells full of flowers holding up a solid brick wall. "That's my favorite," she said. "I can hardly wait to take Frisky over it."

"You were right about the jumps being fancier," Ashleigh said. "And I don't know if I like any of them. They all look kind of scary."

"You haven't tried them yet. You'll do great, I'm sure," Mona reassured her. "Once you and Stardust have gone over a few of them, you won't even think about it. I'm going to get a drink. I'll meet you by the practice ring. Want something?"

Ashleigh shook her head. The thought of eating or drinking anything made her stomach turn. She wished she had Mona's confidence. She was starting to understand why Mrs. Gardener had made such a big deal about her riding in a rated show after only a couple of schooling shows. But no matter how imposing the jumps looked, she was going to do it.

Across the arena, spectators were climbing onto the bleachers. Ashleigh was surprised to see Sam Wiggins walking toward her. What was he doing at a horse show? When he looked across the ring and waved at another rider, Ashleigh looked around to see who waved back.

It was Danielle, on her beautiful black gelding. When Ashleigh looked back, Sam was walking around the show ring. He paused near Danielle and spoke to her, laughing and gesturing with his hands. Then he headed toward Ashleigh, with Danielle and her horse right behind him.

"Danielle Drinan," he said, "I'd like you to meet Ashleigh Griffen. Ashleigh is going to be the world's greatest jockey someday." He glanced at Ashleigh and smiled. "Danielle here is riding one of my favorite retired racehorses. Magic is out of Bold Ruler, Ashleigh."

Ashleigh gasped. "Secretariat's and Royal Tee's sire! I knew he looked familiar. Magic and Aladdin are related!" she exclaimed. "You are so lucky," she told Danielle. "Magic is an awesome horse."

"Thanks," Danielle said. "I love him. If it weren't for Sam and Magic, I wouldn't be riding at all. When my parents had to have my old mare put down last year, I didn't want another horse. My old trainer knew Sam was looking for a home for Magic, so he called him. Magic is so much fun—he can do just about anything."

Riders were entering the arena to practice before the first classes.

"Time for you to warm up," Sam said. "I hope you both do well."

"Good luck," Danielle said to Ashleigh.

"Thanks," Ashleigh replied. "You too."

She hurried back to the trailer to get Stardust and led her over to the warm-up ring. Mona and Frisky were already trotting over a row of cavaletti poles.

Ashleigh mounted up and began to trot around the practice ring. The other competitors looked serious, and the atmosphere was tense. Ashleigh tried to smile as a boy trotted by on a gray gelding, but the boy ignored her. Ashleigh trotted Stardust over the ground poles several times and then headed her for one of the plain rail jumps. They popped over the rail easily, and Ashleigh turned the mare toward a small fence that was painted like a circus tent. It wasn't any higher than the schooling show jumps, but Ashleigh felt as though everyone in the ring were watching her. She tensed her hands on the reins, and Stardust reacted to the pressure on her mouth, flicking her ears back and shortening her stride. Ashleigh released the reins too late, and Stardust took off too close to the jump, popping over it awkwardly.

They clipped the top rail as they went over. Ashleigh cringed as she heard the hollow thunk of the pole hitting the ground. She stopped Stardust and looked back to see a show official replacing the rail.

"Do you really think you can handle the course?"

Ashleigh snapped her head around to see Debbie watching her. Debbie's gray mare was standing with her weight off one foreleg.

"I think your horse is still hurting," Ashleigh said. "You should take her over to the vet."

"You're just afraid of the competition," Debbie said, turning the mare away.

Ashleigh watched the horse walk off. The mare seemed to move all right. She shrugged and turned back to the course. But before they could make another attempt at the jump, the loudspeaker buzzed. The announcer's voice rang out over the show grounds. It was time for the first class.

"Pairs jumping first," Mona said, riding up beside her. "We go second."

Ashleigh pulled up beside Mona and watched the first two riders, a boy and a girl, go through the colorful course. She wished she'd had more time to practice, but the pairs course wasn't very complicated. With Mona and Frisky beside them, she was sure she and Stardust would do fine.

When they rode into the ring, she glanced at Mona. "Let's do it," Mona said, starting Frisky at a canter around the ring.

Ashleigh and Stardust moved up beside them, and they came at the first jump in stride with each other. She tried to concentrate on keeping Stardust in step with Frisky, but in her mind Ashleigh was reliving the jump she had missed during the warm-ups. The sound of the rail hitting the ground kept playing in her head. As they continued around the course each of the jumps seemed to be a greater challenge than the last. *It's just a few jumps,* she told herself. *No big deal.* She gritted her teeth and kept going. Stardust was working well alongside Frisky, but Ashleigh felt as though she was simply along for the ride. She just couldn't relax.

By the time they completed the course, Ashleigh felt drained. But they had ridden a clean round, even if she hadn't enjoyed it very much.

"Are you okay?" Mona asked as they left the ring.

Ashleigh nodded. "I just wasn't ready," she said. "I'll do better in my next class."

When the judging for the pairs class was over, Ashleigh and Mona placed third. Ashleigh rode out of the ring relieved. Stardust had really taken care of her over the course, and she had another ribbon to add to their collection.

She went back to the practice ring, and when the hunter class started, Ashleigh felt ready. She just needed to pay attention to their timing. The class had more than forty competitors; some were really good, but some were having trouble. A couple of the horses balked at the liverpool, running out at the last second. One girl fell off, but she jumped to her feet right away, unhurt.

Ashleigh was one of the last on the program. Stardust grew impatient, pawing the ground and tossing her head. Ashleigh stroked her neck, trying to calm her. "It's all right, girl. We just have to wait our turn."

They watched Mona ride the course, taking Frisky over every one of the jumps with practiced ease. Ashleigh wished she felt as calm and sure as Mona looked. As Mona rode out of the ring, Ashleigh applauded with the crowd. "Way to go!" she called.

When Danielle and Magic went through the course, Ashleigh watched closely. The big black horse sailed over the jumps and seemed to be having the time of his life. But at the brick wall Danielle cued him too soon, and Magic took off too far from the jump. He stretched to clear it but still caught the wall with his back hooves. When the jump fell, Danielle kept going, her eyes on the next obstacle. They finished the course without any more faults, and Danielle rode from the ring with her head high. Ashleigh clapped hard for them.

When her turn finally came, Ashleigh took a deep breath, then exhaled and trotted Stardust into the ring before circling at the canter. Stardust cleared the first flower jump and then the second with no problem, but when they reached the third, the wishing wells, she was off her stride, catching the artificial brick wall as she went over it. Ashleigh winced at the sound of the horse's hooves hitting the wood. She turned Stardust toward the next jump and breathed a sigh of relief when they cleared the green-and-white striped rails. But Ashleigh's reins were getting too long to steer, and she cut her turn to the next brush jump. She gathered up her reins at the last minute, adding a stride to be safe, and Stardust's hooves clipped the rail, sending it to the ground.

By the time she headed Stardust toward the liver-pool, all Ashleigh wanted to do was get out of the ring. She rushed the jump, eager to get the class over with. She braced herself, ready for Stardust to balk, but instead Stardust refused the jump, avoiding the blue tarp altogether. Ashleigh nearly came out of the saddle, grabbing mane and leather to keep her seat. She rode from the arena with her face flushed with humiliation.

"It's okay, Ashleigh," Mona reassured her. "It'll be easier next time. You'll see."

Ashleigh tried to smile, but she wasn't sure if she agreed with Mona. She didn't belong at a rated show.

Ashleigh wasn't surprised when the announcement came that Mona had won first place. Her round had been flawless. Danielle rode out of the ring with a fifth-place ribbon on Magic's headstall. Both girls were smiling. "Just wait," she heard Danielle say to Mona with a grin. "Tomorrow Magic and I are going to give you a run for the blue ribbon."

"I'm sure you will," Mona said, beaming. She stopped Frisky next to Ashleigh and Mona as Danielle rode Magic away.

"Congratulations," Ashleigh said. "You guys make it look easy."

"You'll do better in the equitation class," Mona

said. "You and Stardust make *that* look easy."

Ashleigh didn't even want to ride in the equitation class after her jumping disaster. But she followed Mona and Frisky through the gate. When the announcer began to call out commands, Ashleigh began to feel better. No jumps to worry about—just her and her horse. Stardust settled down and stayed on the rail, responding to each of Ashleigh's cues perfectly. They sailed through the class, and when it came time for the ribbons, she and Stardust left the ring with a red.

"Good girl," she told Stardust as she dismounted. "As long as there are no jumps, we're fine."

Mona walked up, waving her fourth-place ribbon. "That was great, Ash. And tomorrow will be better," she said confidently. "Frisky and I are going to get at least a third in equitation, and you're going to get a ribbon in jumping."

Ashleigh didn't say anything. She still hadn't decided whether or not she'd be showing the next day. She led Stardust toward the Gardeners' trailer and busied herself with Stardust's tack.

Sam Wiggins was standing by the trailer, talking to Mrs. Gardener. "You both did a great job," he said.

Ashleigh looked down. "My jumping was completely embarrassing," she mumbled.

Sam smiled at her and shook his head. "But you

really pulled it together for your equitation class. It takes a lot of courage to try again after you've had a bad ride. You did great, Ashleigh."

"Really?" She hadn't thought she was being very brave.

Sam rubbed Stardust's nose. "You know," he said, "when you're a jockey you may have a lousy race, then have to turn around and ride again. And you can't let that first race ruin the second one. You proved today you can come back and do well. That's important, Ashleigh. I'm glad to see that kind of determination."

"Thanks, Sam," she said.

"I have to get going," he said. "I'll be here tomorrow, so I'll see both of you ride again then."

Ashleigh was quiet during the drive home. Fortunately, Mona was so excited about her win that she chattered happily and didn't seem to notice how little Ashleigh spoke. When they dropped Ashleigh and Stardust off, Mona hung out the truck window. "See you tomorrow morning!" she called, waving good-bye.

Ashleigh put Stardust in her turnout, smiling when the mare walked a few steps, then dropped to the ground and rolled. Her legs flailed in the air as she went all the way over.

"That really took care of your braids," Ashleigh said. "But I bet it felt good."

She watched Stardust scramble to her feet and walk off to where Moe stood at the far end of the paddock, grazing. *Maybe I shouldn't show at all tomorrow,* Ashleigh thought as she stood there. *Stardust looks tired, and we really didn't do very well....*

Jonas was strolling up the lane between the paddocks. "Just checking on fences," he said, stopping at Stardust and Moe's turnout. "I'm surprised you didn't put Stardust in her stall," he said. "It's going to take a lot of work to get her cleaned up again for tomorrow."

Ashleigh gave the stable hand a quick look. "I don't think I'm going to the show tomorrow," she said.

"Didn't it go well today?" Jonas asked.

"Not really," Ashleigh said. "I mean, our flat class was okay, but we didn't do that well in our jumping class." Ashleigh turned away from the paddock, leaning against the rails and looking across the pastures at Edgardale's broodmares.

"Mona must be disappointed," Jonas said.

Ashleigh bit her lip and winced. "She doesn't know yet," she said.

Before Jonas could say anything more, Ashleigh stepped away from the fence. "I know, I'll call her right now." She trudged up to the house, but when she walked inside, Caroline was on the phone.

She held the receiver out to Ashleigh. "Hey, Ash, it's Mona."

Ashleigh took the phone, "I'm glad you called," she began.

But before she could say anything else, Mona broke in. "Can you come over? I have the coolest thing to show you!"

The excitement in Mona's voice got Ashleigh's attention. "What is it?" she asked.

"I have to show you," Mona said. "It's just too awesome, Ashleigh. Can you come over?"

"I'll be right there."

Ashleigh hopped on her bike and pedaled down the driveway, burning with curiosity. What in the world could Mona be so excited about?

9

When Ashleigh rode up the Gardeners' driveway, Mona was waiting on the porch. "Hurry up!" she called, waving a piece of newspaper. "You have to see this!"

As Ashleigh stopped her bike, Mona came down to meet her at the bottom of the steps, holding the paper out. "Look!"

It was the *Bluegrass Almanac,* one of the local papers. When Ashleigh saw the photograph at the top of the page, she gasped. It was a straight-on shot of her and Stardust flying over a jump at the Bluefield show. "Is that really us?" she said. "We look so . . ." Her voice trailed off. She couldn't stop staring at the picture.

"Intense," Mona filled in. She handed Ashleigh the article.

A second photo showed Stardust and Frisky soaring

over a jump in perfect unison in the pairs class at their first schooling show. "Wow!" Ashleigh exclaimed. It was a great picture.

"Isn't that the coolest thing?" Mona asked. "Read the article."

Ashleigh read slowly, savoring the words. "It says, 'Novice Ashleigh Griffen and her partner, Mona Gardener, rode away with the blue in pairs jumping.'" Ashleigh looked at Mona. "This is the coolest, Mona. We got our picture in the paper!"

"If they did an article that big for a schooling show, think of what they'll do for a rated show. Maybe we'll get our picture in the paper again. We're almost famous, Ash," Mona finished with a laugh.

Ashleigh imagined Edgardale's tack room wall covered with photos and articles and all the ribbons she and Stardust would win. "Ashleigh Griffen and Mona Gardener," she said dreamily. "The famous equestrian team from Kentucky, representing the United States at the Olympic Games!" Then she shook her head. "I guess I'd better get home. I still need to get my stalls done." *And get Stardust's mane rebraided,* she thought. No way was she going to miss the show the next day!

"See you in the morning," Mona said.

•   •   •

"You should have seen Peter ride Aladdin today, Ashleigh," Rory said when the family sat down to dinner. "All Aladdin wanted to do was gallop, but Mike told Peter not to let him. He said to make him save it for tomorrow."

Ashleigh glanced at her parents. Her father nodded. "He's ready to run, that's for sure," he said, rubbing his hands together. "It's going to be one hot race tomorrow."

Ashleigh sighed. She still wanted to see Aladdin run, but she had decided to show, and now she was going to have to follow through with it.

After she washed the dishes, she hurried down to the barn to fix Stardust's braids.

On Sunday morning Edgardale was a hive of activity. Ashleigh was busy getting ready for the show, while the rest of the family prepared for their pre-race brunch with the Danworths.

"What do you think of this outfit?" Caroline asked Ashleigh, twirling to show off her short lilac-colored dress.

"Nice," Ashleigh said unconvincingly as she concentrated on fastening the collar of her ratcatcher.

"Mrs. Gardener and Mona are here," her mother

called up the stairs. Ashleigh rushed down the stairs, her boots in her hands.

"We're leaving right away, too," Mrs. Griffen said. "We don't want to be late for brunch with the Danworths." She gave Ashleigh a worried frown. "We won't be home until after you get back from the show, but Jonas will be here in case you need anything."

"That's all right, Mom," Ashleigh said, heading for the door. "I'll be fine."

But when they pulled into the crowded show grounds half an hour later, Ashleigh wished she had changed her mind and gone to the racetrack with her family after all.

It didn't seem possible, but the Sunday show crowd looked even more polished than the riders she had seen the day before. She doubted any press photographer was likely to notice her and Stardust when there were so many perfectly turned-out horses and riders at this show.

She squared her shoulders and tightened her grip on Stardust's lead line. They would just have to make the best of things.

"Ready, Ash?" Mona called from the back of the horse trailer. "Let's get the horses tacked up."

Ashleigh looked at her friend as Mona swung up onto Frisky's back. Mona looked calm and sure of herself, and Frisky looked like the ideal show horse, standing with her graceful neck arched, waiting for Mona to cue her. Her smoothly clipped coat had an iridescent sheen, and each of her braids was tacked neatly along her crest. They looked like a picture of perfect horsemanship.

Stardust shoved at Ashleigh with her nose, and Ashleigh jumped away. "Hey," she cried. "You're going to mess up my jacket!"

"She can't rub you if you're on her back," Mona pointed out.

Ashleigh settled her helmet on her head and climbed onto Stardust's back, trying to block out the bustle and activity around her. But everywhere she looked she saw neatly dressed riders on perfectly groomed horses.

Two boys rode by, their black jackets and tan breeches spotless, their tall boots glistening in the sun. As Ashleigh watched them pass she squirmed, her shoulders sliding under the loose fit of her mother's old jacket. At least Stardust's coat glowed with good health and frequent groomings, Ashleigh reassured herself.

Mona headed for the warm-up ring, and Ashleigh started to follow. But suddenly Stardust gave a loud snort and leaped in the air. Ashleigh found herself grabbing the mare's mane as they hopped sideways. She shortened her reins, getting Stardust under control before the mare could bolt. Stardust kept her neck arched and her head twisted, keeping her eye on a blue banner flapping in the spring breeze.

Ashleigh urged Stardust toward the banner, which snapped and twisted. Stardust snorted again, but this time she stretched her neck and sniffed it.

"You just need to calm down, silly." Ashleigh stroked Stardust's neck. As she spoke she realized she was talking to herself as much as Stardust. Her nervousness was being communicated down the reins to her horse.

"We're not doing very well, are we, Stardust?" she said to the mare. "Maybe we should skip the jumping class and just do the flat."

But then she heard a familiar voice, and she stopped cold.

"After the way she rode yesterday, I'm amazed she showed up today. If I was her, I'd learn to jump before I started showing in A-rated shows."

At the sound of Debbie's voice, Ashleigh's jaw tightened.

"Ashleigh's not so bad, Debbie," she heard Danielle say.

Ashleigh leaned forward, peering around the trailer that blocked her view of the other girls. She saw Danielle sitting on Magic, looking wonderful in her fitted jacket and polished boots. Magic's black coat gleamed in the sunlight. Debbie stood on the ground, holding her mare's reins. The gray was keeping the weight off her right foreleg again. Ashleigh frowned. Didn't Debbie realize her horse was lame?

"Why aren't you getting on?" Danielle asked Debbie.

"Gazelle isn't putting any weight on her leg again," Debbie said. "I thought she'd be better by now, but I'm not going to ride her if she's hurting. I'm waiting for the show vet to check her."

"I hope everything is okay," Danielle said. "But I need to warm Magic up."

"See you later," Debbie said.

Danielle rode toward the warm-up arena. Ashleigh gave a sigh of relief. Debbie did care about her horse after all.

"We're not going to chicken out, Stardust," Asheigh said. She gave the mare a nudge and headed for the warm-up area, too. "We're going to show everyone what you can do."

When they reached the gate to the practice ring, the attendant stopped her.

"You'll have to wait until someone leaves," the woman said. "There are already enough riders in the warm-up ring."

Ashleigh waited by the gate for a minute, watching Mona take Frisky around the practice jumps. Danielle was doing the same with Magic. Both girls looked relaxed and comfortable. But watching only made Ashleigh feel nervous again. She dismounted and started to walk Stardust around while they waited their turn.

Debbie was holding her mare at the show vet's truck. The vet stood up from examining her mare's hoof, shaking his head. He said something to Debbie, who swiped at her eyes with the back of her hand. Then she turned away and led the mare back toward the trailers, walking slowly.

Ashleigh was glad Debbie cared enough about her horse not to push the mare in order to ride in the show. She almost felt sorry for her.

Across the grounds she saw Sam sitting in the bleachers. When she waved to him the ex-jockey rose and limped toward her with his silver-tipped cane.

"Are you ready for today?" Sam asked her with a smile.

Ashleigh shrugged and shook her head unhappily. "I wish I had gone to the track with my family. Now I'm going to miss Aladdin's race."

Sam patted Stardust's neck. "Hard choice to make, huh?"

Ashleigh wrinkled her nose. "Yeah. I think I made the wrong one." No matter how hard she tried to have fun at shows, she always felt out of place. It was nerve-wracking, and though jumping was fun, Ashleigh didn't love it the way Mona and Danielle did.

Danielle cantered past on Magic. She waved to Ashleigh and Sam.

"He looks great, Dani," Sam called. Then he told Ashleigh, "Magic was a rack of bones and afraid of his own shadow when I got him. It took almost a year before he was healthy and rideable again."

A rider walked her horse out of the arena. "I guess it's my turn," Ashleigh said shakily, not at all sure she was ready to jump again.

"Here," Sam said. He stood by Stardust's shoulder and cupped his hands. "Jockeys always get a leg up."

"But I'm not a jockey," Ashleigh reminded him.

Sam gave her a surprised look. "Have you already forgotten you're going to be the world's greatest jockey?"

"No," Ashleigh said with a faint smile, "I haven't forgotten. But this isn't exactly a racetrack." She indicated the show ring full of jumps.

"There's no reason a jockey can't do some jumping, too," Sam said. "Who knows—you may have a knack for steeplechase."

"No way!" Ashleigh laughed. "You won't catch me galloping over those huge jumps!"

She let Sam help her into the saddle. "Thanks, Sam," she said, turning Stardust toward the gate.

"I'll be cheering for you," he replied.

As Ashleigh approached the gate, a girl with a red braid cut in front of her. Ashleigh pulled Stardust to the side in time to avoid colliding with the girl's prancing bay gelding. She glared at the rider's back, but the girl was so busy trying to settle her horse she didn't even notice how close they had come to bumping Stardust.

The horse tossed his head and pawed the ground. He switched his tail and fought the death grip the girl had on the reins. Ashleigh felt sorry for him. Neither the horse nor his rider looked very happy. When the bay danced sideways, almost hitting the fence, the red-haired girl gave him a smack on the shoulder and yanked on the reins.

"That's really going to settle him down," Ashleigh muttered to herself.

"Are you sure you can handle him?" the gate attendant asked the girl. "He looks like he's going to give you some problems."

"He's fine," the girl said, circling the excited gelding. "Just let us into the ring. Once we start working he'll be all right."

"If you're sure . . ." the attendant said. She didn't look convinced, but she opened the gate and the girl rode through.

Ashleigh watched them circle the ring. The horse

did seem to settle down once he got going.

"Sorry about that," the woman at the gate said to Ashleigh.

Ashleigh shrugged. "That's okay. We can wait a little longer." She watched some of the riders take their horses over the jumps. She smiled at Mona as the other girl rode past. "You and Frisky look great," she said.

"Thanks," Mona said. "I'm just going to take Frisky over a couple more, then you can take our place in here. All right?"

"Fine," Ashleigh said. "We'll watch you go." She relaxed in the saddle, watching Mona closely.

From the corner of her eye she saw the bay gelding crow-hop. The red-haired girl pulled on the reins and the gelding stopped still, then tossed its head and kicked out with its hind legs.

"You need to get that horse under control," the gate attendant called to the girl.

Mona was at the far side of the ring, pushing Frisky to a canter. She didn't seem to notice the excited bay, who gave another stiff-legged hop. His rider bounced in the saddle, then hauled his head around until his nose was at her foot.

Mona headed Frisky for a big brush jump. Ashleigh watched closely, but then the girl with the bay distracted her.

"I've got him under control," the girl called to the gate attendant, who was trying to wave her over. The horse swished his tail and pinned his ears, fighting the pull on his bit.

"She doesn't have any control at all," Ashleigh muttered, disgusted.

The attendant swung the gate open and gestured again for the rider to bring her horse out. But instead, the girl gave the horse a quick jab with her heels.

The horse exploded into the air, sending the red-haired girl flying from his back. Then he wheeled away, charging straight toward Mona and Frisky as they approached the jump.

10

Ashleigh gasped in horror as the loose horse startled Frisky, who shied just before she reached the fence. Mona flew from her back. Frisky bounded over the fence riderless and landed right in front of the wild-eyed bay. Ashleigh watched helplessly, waiting for the crash. But the running horse swerved, missing Frisky by inches.

Another rider tried to grab Frisky's bridle, but the mare spun away and headed for the gate. Before the gate attendant could react, Mona's mare darted through the opening.

Ashleigh felt Stardust's muscles bunch as Frisky shot past them. Ashleigh held her in check, but Stardust circled, fighting to follow Frisky in her head-long flight across the show grounds. Around them other horses milled nervously.

Ashleigh snapped her head around in time to see the attendant slam the gate shut before the bay gelding got out, too. Another rider had dismounted and was helping the fallen girl to her feet. She looked more angry than hurt.

Mona was on her feet, and Mrs. Gardener was halfway across the ring. "I'm okay," Mona called to her mother. "Where's Frisky?"

As soon as she knew Mona was all right, Ashleigh turned Stardust. It was easy to track Frisky's path. She could see people scatter as the mare charged through the crowd. The cantering horse darted left and right to avoid the spectators who tried to catch her. All the noise and the lunging people only frightened Frisky more, driving her into a gallop. Ashleigh knew what she had to do.

"Come on, Stardust!" Ashleigh cried. She released the reins and gave the mare a quick rap with her heels. Without a second's hesitation, Stardust broke into a canter. Ashleigh headed her across the field, through the scattered crowd.

She saw a woman grab at Frisky's flapping reins, but Frisky flipped her head, eluding capture. The frantic mare sped up and headed toward the show's makeshift parking lot. Ashleigh sucked in her breath. Beyond the parking lot was a busy road. They had to catch Frisky before she ran right into traffic!

"Let's go!" Ashleigh gave Stardust more rein and urged her into a gallop. Ahead of them, a rail fence blocked the way. Rows of bright spring flowers spilled over the ground in front of it. Stardust had never jumped anything that high, but Ashleigh knew they didn't have time to go around it.

She felt her stomach tighten. The jumps on the show course were designed to give if a horse's hooves hit them. The fence looked higher than the jumps, and if Stardust hit it, she could go down. But Stardust headed gamely for the strange jump. *I just need to trust her,* Ashleigh told herself. *I know Stardust can clear the fence.*

Ashleigh's heart thudded wildly in her chest. She'd never come at a jump from a full gallop. She held her breath and gritted her teeth while she moved into jumping position and focused on her balance.

When Stardust took off, Ashleigh felt as though she had been launched into outer space. The moment of suspension seemed to last an eternity. It was as if they were sailing over the fence in slow motion. There was no sound but the wind whistling past Ashleigh's ears, and the ground looked as if it were miles away. Then Stardust's front hooves touched the ground. As her hind feet hit the grass she bounded away from the jump and they were off again. Ashleigh sat down in the saddle. "Good girl!" she cried, a rush of relief coursing through her.

Frisky's race training seemed to have kicked in. The bay mare stretched out like a greyhound and galloped toward the parked cars at the far end of the show grounds.

"We have to stop her," Ashleigh gasped, urging Stardust to go even faster. Their shortcut over the fence had cut into Frisky's lead, but they still had some distance to make up.

Ashleigh gave Stardust another nudge, but the mare seemed to be giving her all. Ashleigh leaned forward, watching Frisky charge ahead with distance-eating strides, the loose stirrup irons slapping her sides and driving her on. Frisky careened through the rows of cars, then turned onto the fence-lined drive, making a beeline for the road.

"Oh, no!" Ashleigh cried in horror.

It was starting to look hopeless. Frisky was a former racehorse, and she was much faster than Stardust. Then Ashleigh remembered what Sam had told her. A race was won not by the fastest horse but by the horse who ran the best race. Ashleigh had to figure out a way to outrun Frisky, and she had to do it quickly.

At the practice track Meghan had taken up the reins so that Aladdin could brace himself against the bit. *Maybe that would help Stardust!* Ashleigh thought. She leaned forward, taking up more contact with Stardust's mouth. But to Ashleigh's horror, Stardust dropped her speed. Stardust hadn't been trained as a racehorse, and to her, tightened reins meant that her rider wanted her to slow down. Ashleigh quickly loosened the reins and urged her mare to speed up again.

Ashleigh thought desperately about the races she'd seen, and tried to think of what the best jockeys did that she wasn't doing. Then suddenly she remembered Rory's wind-up cars. The car with the upright sail had veered and run into the wall because of wind resistance. It had worked at the science fair, too. Over and over again she had sent the car with the sail off course because of wind resistance. Jockeys crouched as low as possible on the horses' backs as they flew around the track because of wind resistance!

Ashleigh leaned forward over Stardust's shoulders. She brought her head and shoulders low and slid her hands up the mare's neck.

"Come on, girl. We can do this," she called, squeezing Stardust with her legs. Beneath her she felt the mare push even harder. Stardust's muscled neck pumped beneath Ashleigh's fisted hands. The sound of Stardust's hooves pounding on the dirt filled her head.

Stardust's long strides covered the ground so fast that everything seemed a blur to Ashleigh—everything but the runaway mare in front of them.

The distance between Frisky and Stardust closed as Ashleigh kept her mare on a straight route through the parking lot. Her arms ached from clenching the reins. But they couldn't give up. No one else could stop Frisky. It was up to her and Stardust to save Mona's horse.

Then they were on the drive that led from the parking lot to the road. Fences lined both sides of the drive, creating a narrow path. Bright flags atop the posts snapped in the spring breeze. Ashleigh felt a sudden tension in her stomach. The last thing she needed was for Stardust to shy at this speed.

But Stardust was running her heart out, trying to catch up with Frisky.

Ashleigh realized that if a car pulled into the fence-lined drive, there would be no place for the horses to go. There would be no way to avoid a disaster. But she shoved the thought of an accident from her mind. The only thing that mattered was stopping Frisky before the mare reached the road.

A gust of wind made a banner flap, and Frisky skittered across the road in front of them. Ashleigh swallowed a lump of fear. If Frisky spooked again and ran into them, they would all go down hard.

Ashleigh thought of Sam's shattered leg, and she clenched her teeth. She couldn't stop now. She reached her hand out. She could almost touch Frisky.

With the two horses so close together, Ashleigh couldn't tell if the pounding she heard was her heart in her chest or the horses' hooves beating the ground. "We can do this, girl," she called to Stardust, begging her to have a little speed left.

Then they were at Frisky's hip. Ashleigh's ears were filled with the sounds of the horses' breathing, the pounding hooves, and the wind whipping past her ears. She could see the road getting closer with each thundering stride.

"Frisky!" she yelled as loudly as she could. "Whoa, girl!"

Frisky's ears flicked. Her steps faltered slightly, and she slowed a bit. She was listening! The slight distraction helped. Stardust pulled up beside the other horse.

Some of Stardust's braids had come undone, and Ashleigh gripped the mare's loose mane tightly. She leaned over Stardust's shoulder and stretched out her arm, grappling for Frisky's flapping reins. The leather brushed her fingertips, just out of reach, until finally she closed her fist around a rein.

Frisky tossed her head, and Ashleigh clung to Stardust's mane desperately with her other hand.

With a half-ton of weight pulling on her, it took all her balance and strength to keep from flying off Stardust's back. Her arms ached, and she felt dizzy.

Ahead of them Ashleigh could see cars whizzing by on the road. They were getting dangerously close! She gave a firm tug on Frisky's rein, and the mare slowed. Ashleigh tightened her grip on the rein and sat up in the saddle. It took only a few steps to slow both horses to a trot, and finally they stopped, just a few feet from the road. A large truck rumbled by, and Ashleigh sucked in her breath. A few more steps, and both horses would have been in its path.

She released her breath. Stardust was breathing hard. Frisky snorted and tossed her head.

For a minute Ashleigh sat still, catching her breath. She stroked Stardust's neck and gave a shaky laugh. "Why am I out of breath? You guys did all the running."

She leaned over and rubbed Frisky's neck. "Are you done scaring everyone, you big silly?"

As she said it Ashleigh realized she really hadn't been that scared for herself—mostly what had frightened her was the thought that Frisky would get hurt. It had actually felt good to get out of the ring and ride like the wind.

Frisky touched noses with Stardust and released a big, gusty sigh. Stardust bobbed her head, and Ashleigh laughed. "Come on, you two, let's go."

Ashleigh looked over her shoulder. People were crossing the parking lot and hurrying toward them. She circled the horses and headed back to the show ring at an easy walk.

11

"That was amazing!"

"What a ride!"

"Nice going!"

The comments swirled around Ashleigh as she ponied Frisky through the crowd gathered at the edge of the parking lot. She could see Mona and Mrs. Gardener crossing the grounds, and she headed in their direction.

When she reached them, Ashleigh handed Frisky's reins to Mona. Mona flung her arms around the bay mare's neck and looked up at Ashleigh. Her best friend's grateful smile was all the thanks Ashleigh needed.

"That was close," Mona said. "I thought she was going to end up on the road for sure."

"I stopped her just in time," Ashleigh said. "You're okay, right?"

"I'm fine," Mona said. She grinned and rubbed her hip. "There's probably a dent on the ground where I landed, though."

"I don't think I took a breath all this time!" Mrs. Gardener exclaimed. She reached up and squeezed Ashleigh's hand. "You are one gutsy girl," she said. "I don't think anyone else could have outrun Frisky the way you and Stardust did."

Around them, scattered applause broke out. Ashleigh ducked her head, embarrassed by the attention. But the sound of clapping spread until the entire show ground echoed with applause. She sat a little straighter in the saddle and lifted her chin, patting Stardust's shoulder. "Stardust did all the work," she said to Mona.

"You did it together," Mona said.

Sam broke through the crowd, a broad grin on his face. When he reached Ashleigh he slapped her knee. "Mark my words. You were born to be a jockey, kid," he said excitedly.

Ashleigh smiled, a little embarrassed. *That's all I want to do*, she thought. *I just want to race.* But before she could say anything, the loudspeaker hummed again. The announcer's voice carried over the show grounds. "Thanks to Ashleigh Griffen and her mare, Stardust, for averting a disaster. That was a very impressive ride, Ashleigh. And now let's get back to the ring. The show, ladies and gentlemen, must go on."

The crowd laughed and people started heading back to the show ring, where riders were still preparing for their classes.

The show vet arrived as the spectators melted away. He smiled up at Ashleigh and nodded approvingly. "Nice piece of riding back there," he said, then turned to Mona. "Now, let me take a look at your mare."

They looked on anxiously as the vet examined Frisky's legs. He had Mona walk and trot her while he watched, then he bent down to run his hands along her legs again. In a minute he rose. "This horse is fine," he said. "If you want to continue in the show, you have my approval."

Mona smiled with relief. "Thank you," she said.

The vet held Frisky's bridle while Mona swung onto the mare's back. "I wouldn't recommend any more mad gallops for a while, though," he said, winking at Mona.

"Don't worry!" she replied. She glanced at Ashleigh. "I need to take her back to the ring, Ash. See you in a few minutes."

The vet turned to Ashleigh as Mona rode away. "Let me check your mare over," he said, stroking Stardust's sleek neck. "This little lady really made some great moves back there."

"She sure did," Ashleigh said proudly, dismounting. It felt strange to be back on the ground.

Sam held Stardust's head. When the vet was done checking her over, he turned to Ashleigh.

"She's fine, too," he said. "You're free to ride her in your classes. And now I have a couple of other horses to look at, if you'll excuse me."

"Thank you," Ashleigh called after him as the vet walked away.

"Do you want a leg up?" Sam asked.

Ashleigh shook her head. "I think I'm done for the day," she said. "Stardust already put in her show."

Sam looked from Ashleigh to Stardust, then back again. He didn't look surprised. "That was quite a race the two of you ran," he said. "I'll walk her out for you if you want to go talk to Mona."

"Thanks, Sam." Ashleigh headed for the show ring, where Mona was walking Frisky before they tried any more jumps.

"Where's Stardust?" Mona asked.

Ashleigh waved Mona over to the fence. "I quit," she said happily.

Mona's jaw dropped. "Quit? But you still have two classes."

Ashleigh laughed. "I still want to jump with you and Frisky for fun, but I'll never be a real show jumper, Mona. That's your thing. I'm going to be a jockey."

"Will you still come to watch me show?" Mona asked.

"Will you come to the track to watch me race?" Ashleigh grinned at her.

Mona nodded. "You know I will."

Ashleigh walked over to where Mrs. Gardener was standing, watching the activity inside the ring. "I hope you don't mind, but I want to scratch my classes," she said.

Mrs. Gardener gave her a concerned frown. "I hope it isn't because of that little episode with the girl and the bay horse," she said. "They were removed from the classes, so you don't have to worry about that happening again."

Ashleigh shook her head. "No," she said quickly. "I like jumping for fun, but showing like this just isn't what I want to do."

Mrs. Gardener's look turned to one of understanding. "You'd better go take your name off the rosters," she said as the announcer called for the start of the class.

Ashleigh headed for the registration booth.

"Hey, Ashleigh, wait up."

She stopped and looked around to see Debbie walking toward her. "Hi," she said, eyeing the other girl suspiciously.

Debbie gave her a thin smile. "I just wanted to say

I'm sorry. I was pretty mean to you. You really are a great rider."

Ashleigh shrugged. "Thanks," she said. "Is your mare okay?"

Debbie dropped her gaze. "The vet says she's probably got a cracked coffin bone. We have to get some X rays taken. Special shoes might help, but she won't be jumping for a long time . . . maybe never."

"I'm sorry she's hurt," Ashleigh said. "I'm not going to do any more jumping, either."

"You're not quitting because of me, are you?" Debbie looked genuinely upset.

Ashleigh quickly shook her head. "Oh, no!" She smiled at Debbie. "I just have other stuff I'd rather do."

"You could be a jockey," Debbie said. "You sure looked like one when you were racing after that mare."

"Maybe," Ashleigh replied.

Sam caught up with her at the registration booth, where she waited for the officials to approve a refund of her show fees.

"Stardust is tied at the Gardeners' trailer," he said. "I found a nice full hay net for her to munch on. She looked pretty content when I left her."

"Thanks for taking care of her, Sam." Ashleigh turned to the booth as a stern-looking man approached the counter.

"We don't normally refund fees when competitors scratch from their classes," he said.

"Oh." Ashleigh dropped her chin.

"But under the circumstances," the man said, a tiny smile straining the corners of his dour mouth, "we feel an exception is quite appropriate."

"Thank you," Ashleigh said, stuffing the money in her jacket pocket.

"You know," the man continued, looking down at her, "you should consider training as a jockey. You certainly looked like you knew what you were doing."

Before she could say anything, he turned away.

Sam tipped his head and grinned at her. "You do have natural ability, Ashleigh. It may take you a while to get the good mounts, but you belong on a Thoroughbred's back, on the track.

"Mona and Danielle are showing in the next class," he continued. "Want to watch them?" He started to walk off, and she hurried to join him.

"Do you mean it?" she demanded.

"Mean what?" Sam gave her a blank look. "That Mona and Danielle are in the next class? I'm sure they are."

"No!" Then Ashleigh caught the twinkle in Sam's eye. "You're teasing me. Do you mean it that I have natural ability?"

Sam stopped and turned to face her. This time his

expression was dead serious. "Ashleigh," he said, "I have been around the track all my life. I've watched people start out as grooms and exercise riders, people who have a passion for the horses and would love nothing better than to have a chance to ride in a race. But lots of them just don't have that little extra something. Then there are the riders whose names are listed with the Triple Crown–winning horses, the riders who can take a good horse and make it great. You have that something, Ashleigh. Don't let it go to waste."

Ashleigh walked toward the bleachers in a happy daze. She sat beside Sam on the riser, waiting for the twelve-and-under jumping class to begin.

Danielle and Magic went through the hunter course without a single fault. Ashleigh and Sam stood and clapped for them as they rode off the course. But Mona and Frisky made it look effortless. Their timing was perfect, with Frisky jumping in a smooth arc over each obstacle.

"You'd never know that just a few minutes ago she was a wild runaway horse, would you?" Sam joked as Mona and Frisky left the ring.

"They were great," Ashleigh said, applauding loudly. When Mona took first place in the twelve-and-under division, Ashleigh clapped even harder. Danielle rode away with second place.

Ashleigh hurried down to the gate to meet Mona.

"You looked perfect!" she cried.

"Thanks, Ash," Mona called happily as she handed her ribbon to her mother and turned Frisky back into the ring to ride in the flat class.

When the flat class started, Ashleigh, Sam, and Mrs. Gardener stayed at the gate to watch. Mona looked good, but Danielle and Magic were the ones who shone. There were a lot of riders, and the judge was thorough, watching each one closely. Ashleigh chewed her lower lip as the judge finally asked the riders to line their horses up in the center of the ring.

Ashleigh wished there could have been two winners. But Mona looked happy with the second-place ribbon the judge clipped to Frisky's bridle, and Danielle's face glowed when the blue ribbon went on Magic's headstall. Mrs. Gardener took an instant camera out of her purse and snapped a picture of her beaming daughter.

Sam looked at his watch as the riders were coming out of the ring. "I'm going to run down to Keeneland now," he said. "The afternoon races are about to start."

Ashleigh whirled around to face him. Maybe she wouldn't have to miss Aladdin's race after all! "Can I go with you?" she asked.

Sam nodded. "Sure."

Ashleigh turned to Mona's mother. "Would it be all right if—"

Mrs. Gardener smiled. "I'll get Stardust home safe and sound, Ashleigh. And Jonas will be there to help me, so don't worry."

"Thank you!" Ashleigh cried. "Let's go!" she said eagerly to Sam.

"Hold on," Sam said. "We've got some congratulating to do first."

They met Mona and Danielle as they rode out of the ring.

"Congratulations, Mona," Ashleigh called.

"Nice riding, Danielle," Sam said.

Mona smiled at Danielle, who rode up beside her. "Frisky and I are going to do a lot of practicing, so don't think we're going to let you take too many blues home."

"What do you mean?" Danielle laughed. "You can't have all the firsts, you know."

"I'm leaving with Sam," Ashleigh interrupted hurriedly, explaining, "We're going to Keeneland."

"All right, Ash," Mona said. "Cheer Aladdin on for me, too, okay?"

"And me," Danielle added. "If he's a relative of Magic's, he has to be a great horse."

"I will, I promise," Ashleigh said. She followed Sam to his truck, and soon they were heading down the dirt drive where Ashleigh had made her wild ride to save Frisky. As they drove between the white rail fences Ashleigh relived the tense few minutes of her exciting gallop down that same drive.

Sam's truck rattled onto the road. Ashleigh leaned forward on her seat, wishing he would speed up. Just then all she wanted was the chance to see Aladdin run in the Keeneland Mile. But when she glanced at the clock on the dashboard, Ashleigh gasped. His race would be starting in just a few minutes! How would they ever make it?

12

Ashleigh cast Sam an anxious look. "Maybe you should go just a little faster."

"We'll make it, I promise," Sam reassured her.

Ashleigh sat back, her feet drumming a steady tattoo on the floor. *Hurry, hurry,* she chanted to herself. *Oh, please don't let us miss the race.*

She sighed with relief when they finally passed the airfield, but when she saw the public parking at the track, she groaned. "Oh, no! The signs say the lots are all full. There's no place to park. The races will be over by the time we get inside."

But Sam didn't seem too concerned about the full lot. He pulled up in front of the entrance to the grandstand and stopped the truck at the curb.

"That sign said unauthorized vehicles will be towed," Ashleigh pointed out.

"I know," Sam said, and climbed from the truck.

Ashleigh jumped out. "Your truck could get towed. Don't you mind?"

But Sam walked up to the ticket booth without seeming too concerned. Ashleigh hurried after him, growing more curious by the moment.

"Good to see you, Sam," the man in the booth said. He gave a slight jerk of his head, and a young woman with Keeneland Valet embroidered on her brightly colored T-shirt approached them.

"May I take your keys, sir?" She held out her hand. Ashleigh watched, astounded, as Sam handed the woman the keys. The valet hopped in the truck and drove away, leaving Ashleigh to stare after the departing vehicle. When Ashleigh turned back, the man at the counter was waving them through the gate. "Come back when you can visit for a few minutes, Sam," he said. "Enjoy the races."

Sam glanced at his watch, then held it up for Ashleigh to see. "We still have time before the horses for the Keeneland Mile go into the viewing paddock," he told Ashleigh. "Let's go over to the backside and take a look around."

She hurried beside Sam as he worked his way through the crowd.

"Hey, Sam! Sam Wiggins!"

Sam stopped as a man rushed up to them.

"I've been looking all over for you." The man had a gruff voice, but his eyes twinkled with good humor. "I need your advice on a colt I'm looking at."

"Ashleigh," Sam said, "I'd like you to meet J. L. Freeman, one of the best trainers in the business."

Ashleigh swallowed hard. "I've seen your picture in the *Daily Racing Form*. You trained Rowdy Dude and Elegant Della," she said. "I've watched them run. They're both fantastic."

The famous trainer grinned at her. "I'm hoping Rowdy's foals will follow in his footsteps," he said. "I'd like to have a few more just like him."

"Ashleigh here is going to be a jockey," Sam told the white-haired trainer. "You should see this kid on a horse."

"Good, huh?" J. L. Freeman stroked his white beard and gazed at Ashleigh again.

"She has more guts and determination than I've seen in a long time," Sam said. "And she has a way with the horses."

Ashleigh couldn't believe Sam was talking about her.

"If Sam is giving you a reference, I know I'll have some rides for you." The trainer dug into his pocket and held out a white business card. "Give me a call when you're ready to do some exercise riding. We'll start you out right."

Ashleigh took the card. "Yes, sir," she said. "I'll call you."

As they headed toward the backside several other people stopped Sam. Soon Ashleigh's head was swimming with the names of trainers, jockeys, and owners. In a short time she had shaken hands with half a dozen people she'd only read about in racing periodicals. And to every person they met, Sam made a point of introducing her as a future jockey. "Watch for this girl on the track," he said again and again. "Ashleigh Griffen is a name to remember."

Ashleigh felt as though her feet weren't even touching the ground as they made their way to the backside. She drifted along in a cloud of happiness, trying to commit every conversation to memory.

"You sure know a lot of people," she commented as they reached the shed rows.

"Yeah, well, that's part of being around the track so long," Sam said. "You'll get used to it."

Ashleigh hoped not. The feeling of being part of something so big and exciting was wonderful. She didn't ever want to take it for granted.

They stepped to the side as grooms led prancing horses down the aisles, their colorful sheets rustling. Other grooms bustled around with pieces of tack and grooming buckets, their arms loaded with leg wraps. Trainers and jockeys conferred in corners. Everywhere she looked, there were people working, and a dazzling Thoroughbred was at the center of every bit of hushed activity. Ashleigh glanced into each stall, admiring the beautiful animals that were the focus of so much attention.

When they reached Aladdin's stall, Mike and Peter had the colt out of his stall. "We're almost ready to take him to the receiving barn for his vet check," Mike said, nodding to Ashleigh and Sam. He stooped to run his hands down Aladdin's front legs.

"I didn't think you were coming today," Peter said as he held Aladdin's head, running his hand along the colt's crest.

"I couldn't miss Aladdin's race," Ashleigh answered. She reached up to rub Aladdin's nose. When he dropped his head and sniffed her, she kissed his black cheek. "Run fast, you big moose," she whispered, inhaling his horsy scent. "Show them all what you can do."

Mike held up Aladdin's bridle with the shadow roll in place. "Let's hope this does the trick again," he said.

Ashleigh grinned. "It'll work," she said confidently.

"I think you're right," Mike said. "And with a little luck, everything else will fall into place, too," he said, frowning slightly. "We drew the number four position. That isn't so bad, but I've watched the number five horse work. He has a tendency to swerve in. His jockey, Tom Connell, doesn't seem to take much control. I don't want Aladdin getting cut off, but I don't want him rushing to the front, either. We have Zach Jackson riding him today. He's a good rider. I just hope he does his job right."

"So did you tell the jockey to hold him back?" Ashleigh asked. "I mean, Aladdin's a come-from-behind kind of horse."

Mike narrowed his eyes, and Ashleigh clamped her mouth shut when she realized she was giving advice to a professional trainer. "Sorry," she murmured.

But Mike was smiling and shaking his head. "Yes, ma'am, I told him, and I'll tell him again when we mount up in the paddock. Come on, Peter. It's time to take him to the receiving barn."

Peter and Mike headed down the aisle with Aladdin, and Sam and Ashleigh started back to the grandstand.

"See you in the winner's circle," Ashleigh called after them.

A crowd was gathered at the viewing paddock, where the fillies for one of the claiming races were being saddled. Ashleigh pointed at a black horse with a white star. "That's Bold's Dark Star," she said to Sam. "My parents put a claim on her."

"She's a nice-looking horse," Sam said.

Mr. and Mrs. Griffen were on the far side of the

viewing paddock. They waved, but the throng around the paddock was too thick to reach them.

When the horses were paraded out of the paddock, Sam was waylaid by another trainer. Mr. and Mrs. Griffen got through the crowd, and Sam gestured to Ashleigh to go on without him. "I'll see you later," he said.

"Ashleigh?" her mother said curiously, wrapping her arm around her daughter's shoulder. "What are you doing here?"

"Sam was at the show," Ashleigh began to explain. "He brought me. Stardust is going home with Mona. Frisky ran away and I caught her—Stardust ran so fast. And Mona won!" she babbled breathlessly.

"Well, I didn't understand any of that, but I'm glad you're here," her father said, laughing. "You're just in time to see the Bold Ruler filly run."

Ashleigh and her parents squeezed up to the rail to watch the claiming race. When the fillies exploded out of the gate, Ashleigh felt the ground rumble beneath her. She longed to be on one of the running horses, and leaned forward, imagining she was astride Dark Star as she followed the filly around the track.

The race was over almost as quickly as it started, and the black filly came in third.

But her parents didn't look disappointed. "Like you said, Ash, she's a distance horse," her father said.

"When they get to the finish line in these sprints, she's just getting started. I think we got her. But let's get up to the grandstand before we miss Aladdin's race."

Caroline and Peter were already in their seats, with Rory between them. Peter patted an empty seat beside him, and Ashleigh slipped into it. Her parents joined Mr. and Mrs. Danworth, who were sitting a row back.

"Glad you could make it, Ash. They're just getting ready for the post parade," Peter said, his voice strained with excitement. "Aladdin looks really good. Mike says he's never been in a better frame of mind."

"Probably from spending time at Edgardale," Mr. Danworth said from behind them.

"That's what Mike said," Peter replied.

As the horses were led single file past the grandstand, Ashleigh's attention was riveted on the track. Some of the Thoroughbreds seemed to be expending all their energy dancing along beside the pony horses, lunging around and fighting their jockeys. When Aladdin came onto the track, he looked alert but calm, moving with restrained energy.

Ashleigh turned to look at the board, where the odds for each horse in the race were posted. Aladdin's odds were terrible.

"Look at his odds!" she exclaimed, pointing at the electronic board. "He's twenty to one. That can't be right."

"Don't worry, Ashleigh," her mother said from behind her. "Those numbers will keep changing right up to the start of the race."

Even as she spoke, the digital readout changed, dropping Aladdin's odds to 8–1.

The number five horse had its ears pinned and kept nipping at the pony horse. Ashleigh shook her head. "That's no good," she said. "I wish he wasn't next to Aladdin."

Peter watched the feisty bay stallion try to wheel around to kick at the pony horse. "Luck of the draw," he said. "Zach said he'll hold Aladdin back and keep him out of the crush."

"He looks so good," Ashleigh said as Aladdin was ponied along the backstretch. The pony rider took the colt around another horse who had stopped on the track and was rearing and kicking.

Peter nodded. "He's saving all his energy for the race."

When the horses reached the starting gate, Aladdin walked right into his slot. Around him, some of the other horses fought their handlers, rearing, their necks lathered in nervous sweat. But Aladdin had never had trouble with the gate.

As soon as the last horse was loaded, the starting bell sounded, the gates flew open, and the announcer's voice blasted from the loudspeakers: "They're off!"

Ashleigh jumped out of her seat, straining to keep track of Aladdin. But he was caught in the midst of the crowd.

"Get him out of the pack!" she yelled, as if the jockey could hear her.

"Felony Fine breaks away at the gate, with Secure Future right behind him." The race announcer's voice carried over the roar of the crowd. "It's number two, Felony Fine, to the inside. They've set a breakneck pace right from the start. Secure Future is holding a strong second, and it's anybody's guess as to who could be in third."

Ashleigh could feel the horses' hooves thundering on the track, and she wished she were standing at the rail rather than in the grandstand. She inhaled deeply, as if she could help Aladdin breathe, and felt her muscles strain as though she were running the race with him.

"Now it's Allocation in third, with Seattle's Smoke coming up from behind."

Where's Aladdin? Ashleigh craned her neck, trying to sort out the big colt from the rest of the fast-moving crush of horses streaming around the turn. Then she saw the number four on his saddle pad. Aladdin was caught in the middle of the pack, with no way out!

She kept her fists clenched, her eyes glued to the

mass of horses that was running a few strides behind the leaders.

"Oh, no!" she cried as the number five horse, Breezy Daze, veered toward Aladdin. Ashleigh's breath locked in her throat. Were they going to crash? There was no place for Aladdin to go. A wreck seemed inevitable. Ashleigh's heart thundered in her chest.

She saw a small opening as another horse dropped back. Zach Jackson must have seen it at the same time, because he steered Aladdin toward it. The jockey angled the speeding colt's nose into the gap, narrowly avoiding a collision with Breezy Daze.

Ashleigh exhaled, feeling dizzy with relief. Aladdin was okay and was out of the crush, but now he had to get up some speed to catch up with the leaders.

"It's Allocation moving into second, and Aladdin's Treasure is moving into third." The jockeys flapped their whips and urged their horses on as they headed toward home. "Allocation is closing the gap, with Aladdin's Treasure right behind," the announcer went on.

Suddenly Aladdin seemed to find another gear and was surging up on Allocation. The announcer's voice rose as the horses galloped on. "Now Felony Fine and Allocation are neck and neck. These two horses are matching each other stride for stride! But Aladdin's Treasure is moving up on the leaders!"

"No! It's too soon!" Ashleigh shrieked. She knew

that Aladdin's best speed came when he was running from behind; if he got out in front, he might get lazy.

Ashleigh stared at the black stallion, who looked like a locomotive roaring down the track. If only he could keep up that pace, Aladdin had the race. He would be in the winner's circle in minutes.

"Go! Go, Aladdin! Come on, boy!" she yelled as Felony Fine dropped back and Aladdin moved nose to nose with Allocation, the lead horse. *Go on, go on,* Ashleigh chanted mentally as they came into the home stretch. But Aladdin seemed to realize he was in the lead, and he relaxed. Ashleigh grimaced as he slowed his pace just enough to lose his edge.

The jockey flicked the whip past Aladdin's eye. The colt picked up speed again, but it was too late. Allocation moved across the finish line a stride ahead of Aladdin, who finished an easy second, with Felony Fine in third.

Ashleigh released the breath she'd been holding for the last several seconds. "If he'd only held him back a while longer," she said, shaking her head. But she knew in her heart that Aladdin had run a great race.

"It was close," Peter replied. "Hey, look, there's Sam," he added, pointing.

The ex-jockey was making his way through the grandstand. When he reached their seats, Mr. Danworth rose and extended his hand. "Good to see you, Sam."

"That was an exciting race," Sam said. "Aladdin ran well."

"We're disappointed that he didn't win, but I agree, he did run a good race," Mr. Danworth replied.

Sam turned to Ashleigh. "I wanted to take you down to talk with Mike and Zach. I always learn a lot when I talk to jockeys and trainers right after the race, while it's still fresh in their minds."

Ashleigh jumped to her feet, looking at her parents for permission.

"We're going to go see about Bold's Dark Star—it looks like we're going to bring her home," her father said. "We'll meet you at Aladdin's stall when we're ready to go."

"I'll come with you," Peter said to Sam, and they turned to make their way down through the stands.

Ashleigh followed Sam and Peter through the crowd, her mind whirring happily. She had gotten to see Aladdin run a great race, and they would be leaving with a new mare for the farm. It was better than any blue ribbon or any picture in the paper. Showing with Mona had been fun, but Ashleigh could take it or leave it. This was where she belonged: at the racetrack, surrounded by Thoroughbreds and the people who loved them.

Peter took Aladdin's reins, while Mike, Sam, and the jockey stood to one side. Aladdin shook his elegant black head, spraying lather every which way. Ashleigh laughed and reached up to stroke the colt's sweaty forehead.

"Hey, Ashleigh," Peter said, "I'll give you a leg up." He bent down and cupped his hands, looking up at her expectantly.

Ashleigh stared at him in shock. Peter was offering to give her a leg up onto Aladdin!

"Go on," he said.

Ashleigh gathered up Aladdin's reins and swung up onto his back. She put her feet in the stirrups and crouched low over his withers, smiling happily down at Peter. Aladdin shook his mane, and Ashleigh patted his neck. It felt wonderful to be on the stallion's back again.

"Ashleigh Griffen," Sam called from behind her, "I want you to meet Zach Jackson. Ashleigh's going to give you a run for your money someday," he told the jockey.

He's right, Ashleigh thought as she turned Aladdin and walked him toward them. *One day I'll give them all a run for their money!*

MARY NEWHALL ANDERSON spent her childhood exploring back roads and trails on horseback with her best friend. She now lives with her husband, her horse-crazy daughter, Danielle, and five horses on Washington State's Olympic Peninsula. Mary has published novels and short stories for both adults and young adults.

THOROUGHBRED

If you enjoyed this book, then you'll love reading all the books in the THOROUGHBRED series!

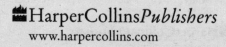

THOROUGHBRED

#23: *Cindy's Honor*   0-06-106493-9

#22: *Arabian Challenge*   0-06-106492-0

#21: *Wonder's Champion*   0-06-106491-2

#20: *Champion's Spirit*   0-06-106490-4

#19: *Cindy's Heartbreak*   0-06-106489-0

#18: *Glory's Rival*   0-06-106398-3

#17: *Ashleigh's Farewell*   0-06-106397-5

#16: *Glory in Danger*   0-06-106396-7

#15: *Glory's Triumph*   0-06-106277-4

#14: *Cindy's Glory*   0-06-106325-8

#13: *Cindy's Runaway Colt*   0-06-106303-7

#12: *Shining's Orphan*   0-06-106281-2

#11: *Wonder's Sister*   0-06-106250-2

#9: *Pride's Challenge*   0-06-106207-3

#8: *Sierra's Steeplechase*   0-06-106164-6

#7: *Samantha's Pride*   0-06-106163-8

#6: *Wonder's Yearling*   0-06-106747-4

#5: *Ashleigh's Dream*   0-06-106737-7

#4: *Wonder's Victory*   0-06-106083-6

#3: *Wonder's First Race*   0-06-106082-8

#2: *Wonder's Promise*   0-06-106085-2

#1: *A Horse Called Wonder*   0-06-106120-4

All books are
$4.50 U.S./$5.50 Canadian